ALONG THE TONTO RIM

Dick Lazarus and his gang are feared on both sides of the Rio Grande. Lazarus's increasingly daring crimes see him raid the ranchero of the Robles family in Mexico, stealing a herd of horses and taking a hostage — Luis Robles — who should fetch a hefty ransom. Dan Calloway, owner of the stolen herd and Luis's friend, is determined to rescue Luis and regain his possessions. Ignoring the warnings, and with an unexpected ally on his side, he pursues Lazarus across the Rio Grande, and along the Tonto Rim . . .

6.1.20

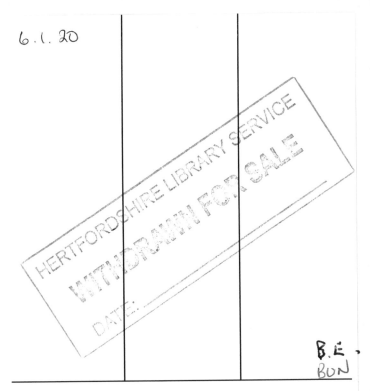
B.E.
BON

Please renew or return items by the date shown on your receipt

www.hertfordshire.gov.uk/libraries

Renewals and enquiries: 0300 123 4049

Textphone for hearing or 0300 123 4041
speech impaired users:

L32 11.16 ✗✱✗

Hertfordshire

WILL DuREY

ALONG THE TONTO RIM

Complete and Unabridged

LINFORD
Leicester

First published in Great Britain in 2015 by
Robert Hale Limited
London

First Linford Edition
published 2019
by arrangement with
The Crowood Press
Wiltshire

A catalogue record for this book is available
from the British Library.

ISBN 978–1–4448–4236–4

Published by
F. A. Thorpe (Publishing)
Anstey, Leicestershire

Set by Words & Graphics Ltd.
Anstey, Leicestershire
Printed and bound in Great Britain by
T. J. International Ltd., Padstow, Cornwall

This book is printed on acid-free paper

1

The high, whitewashed wall which surrounded the little town of San Miguel had long ago been constructed of clay bricks by the God-fearing people who had lived and worked in that area. As he approached it, the American reduced the pace of his big black stallion, slowing it from a canter to a walk. He could feel it shiver and, even though night had now closed around them, he could see flecks of foam slip away from his mount's shoulders to dissipate on the dry ground below. He manoeuvred the big animal towards an arched opening in the wall; beyond was a congregation of small adobe buildings that were homes to the Mexican citizens. It was clear that there had been no grand design as to the layout of the town, the site of each single-level house had been decided in a haphazard fashion, but by common consent, at its centre, around a well with a circular, three-feet-high wall, the area was inviolate. This was the marketplace, a space for trading when the sun wasn't high and for siesta when it was.

One side of the marketplace was dominated by the mission building from which the town had taken its name. Before Texas rebelled against the rule of Mexico this mission had flourished, but now, like most of those that remained in the immediate area of the west bank of the Rio Grande, it was a ruin. The darkness, however, hid from the American's sight its decrepit walls as it towered over the smaller adobe homes like a benevolent guardian.

By the time the American reached this marketplace he had seen no one. Here and there low lights had shown at some of the windows but no curious faces had appeared to witness his progress through the town. He knew, however, that his arrival would not have passed unobserved. He understood the people in these small communities: unwilling, perhaps afraid, to confront strangers until they knew their business and the threat they brought with them.

For an instant he caught the sound of chords strummed on a guitar, but as suddenly as they were played they stopped so that once again the only noise was that created by his own horse's hoofs on the hard ground. A door was open in a building to his right and lights flickered from within. He dismounted and tied the horse to a rail outside that building. Above the door in fading letters was a single word. CANTINA. The smell of spiced meat was so strong that it almost made his eyes water, but he was hungry and the chance of finding an alternative eatery was remote. He stepped inside and paused.

The space within was larger than he expected, a dozen tables were scattered around the room in the same haphazard fashion as the houses around the marketplace. The lack of noise, the absence of conversation or music, had ill-prepared the American for the presence of almost two dozen customers, but these men were mostly peons, land-workers whose skin had become brown and wrinkled from long, hot days in the sun. No one looked at him although it was obvious that they were aware that a stranger, an American, had stepped into their world. Either they kept their heads bowed over the small glasses of tequila or they studied the pieces on the chequered boards in use at some of the tables. All were careful not to look at the newcomer as though an ill-judged movement might give offence. They were silent, as though waiting for the American to unveil the depth of tyranny he'd brought with him.

At the back of the room a girl in a plain green top above a flared black-and-green patterned skirt sat with a guitar across her knees. Her head was high in a proud, fiery manner, a striking contrast to the subservient attitude of the men at the other tables. She looked at the stranger once, a brief but scrutinizing glance which lingered longest on the big Colt that was holstered against his right thigh. No other man in the room was armed. Her eyes, almost as black and shiny as her hair, which was tight to her head and secured in a coil at the back by means of a green comb, conveyed a handful of messages none of which signified he was welcome. Eventually she looked down at the strings of her guitar and strummed soft notes.

Off to his right the American perceived a short and ill-constructed serving counter. As he stepped towards it he could see that it was no cleaner than it was sturdy. Spillages had been left to dry into the wood, leaving barely an inch that wasn't unstained. A cockroach, almost two inches long, skittered unmolested from behind an empty bottle, over the fingers of the man behind the bar before disappearing behind a wooden tray laden with grimy glasses. The man was small and round with a slim moustache, his dark hair was thinning into long strands which looked like painted lines across his head. As he watched the approaching American a forced smile appeared on his face and he spoke quickly as though covering up his nervousness. In accompaniment to his words he retrieved a bottle from a bench behind the counter in anticipation of a customer's need.

'Tequila, *señor*? The very best from Monterrey.'

'Food first,' declared the American, 'then I want a room.'

'A room, *señor*?' The smile disappeared, intimating that only trouble could come from the protracted presence of a gringo on his premises. 'You intend to stay the night?'

'You have rooms that aren't in use.'

The American's words weren't a question and the cantina owner's agreement with the statement was confirmed by his eyes shifting, involuntarily, towards a beaded entranceway at the back of the room. But the betrayal of his own wish to speed the stranger on his way registered on his face. A glint of fear flashed in his eyes, then he extended his arms in a silent plea, as though trying to explain that any profit made from the conduct of legitimate business wouldn't compensate for the trouble it would bring. Although the American noted the other's behaviour he showed no sympathy.

'I'll take the nearest room,' he announced, 'but first bring me some food.'

'*Señor*,' began the owner, the word pleading for understanding, but it was clear that the American had no intention of quitting either the cantina or San Miguel this night. Following a forlorn glance around the room, as though hoping for some assistance from his customers, the owner pushed aside a curtain and disappeared into the room behind.

Shifting the curtain caused a further waft of spiced air to assail the

American's senses, so he turned his back on the bar and stood for a moment to re-examine the room. If the peons had moved at all since he'd entered, it had only been to grasp their small glasses so that the contents could be hastily thrown to the back of their throats if it became necessary to quit the cantina swiftly. Still they didn't look directly at the American, or barely at each other. Their gazes were fixed on the tables around which they sat.

The American switched his attention to the girl. She was young, no more than twenty, and the rough material of her clothes only highlighted the soft and pampered texture of her dark skin. She was beautiful in the way that only Mexican girls can be, completely feminine and tender at one moment but fiery and passionate the next; either gentle and loving with every inch of their being, or dangerous and cruel to those who showed enmity. The American was surprised by his reaction to her and annoyed to find that he had been so wrapped up in his examination of her that he had failed to notice that she had raised her head to look at him. The expression on her face was severe

'Look somewhere else,' she told him.

He walked across the room and sat at the table nearest to her.

'You play that guitar?'

'When I choose to.'

'Now would be a good time to choose to,' he told her.

Her response was almost a sneer and she stood the guitar against the wall to emphasize the fact that she wouldn't play at his bidding. She turned her head to watch the owner, who was hurrying in their direction with a plate of hot food, its aroma preceding it to the place where the American sat.

'I'll need a beer with that,' the American told his host as the plate was put in front of him.

'*Si, señor.*'

'And music might help, too. Get your girl to play something.'

The Mexican spread his arms in a

gesture of hopelessness, as though the slightest task was beyond his capability. 'She's not my girl, *señor*.'

The American paused in raising the forkful of stew that was destined for his mouth. 'You don't employ her?'

'No, *señor*.'

'Is she your daughter?'

'No, *señor*.'

'Who is she?'

'I don't know, *señor*.' That last answer was followed by his tongue swiftly passing across his lips, wetting them, attempting to wash away the lie. The American saw it, understood it and turned his head so that he could study the girl's face.

'She came in here two nights ago,' explained the Mexican. 'Sometimes she eats, sometimes she plays her guitar but mostly she just sits. She's no trouble.'

The expression on the girl's face declared her objection to their discussion as eloquently as her words.

'It's not his business to know why I'm here.'

'If you'd played a tune or danced a few steps while I was eating,' said the American, 'perhaps then you wouldn't have aroused my interest.'

'I play and dance for friends, not gringo *bandidos*.'

Another forkful of spiced food went into the American's mouth.

'*Bandido!*' He spoke as he chewed. 'If that be the case you'd better be careful I don't just shoot you for the fun of it.' His gun came out of its holster so swiftly that the startled girl almost gasped, but instantly she regained her composure and tilted her head a little higher in defiance. The American spun the weapon on his finger and replaced it in the holster.

Simultaneously, as though obeying a command, two of the peons drained the tequila from their glasses and hurried out of the building.

The moment of silence was broken by the Mexican proprietor. 'No trouble, señor,' he pleaded. 'This is a quiet town.'

The American expected another sweep of the Mexican's lips with his tongue but it didn't happen; any conscience he might have had about telling lies had been completely over-shadowed by the rapidity with which the pistol had been drawn and, consequently, the threat to his liveli-hood made manifest by the presence of such a gunman in San Miguel. Instead, his eyes, wide and fear-filled, were fixed on the girl, a look that begged forgiveness, telling her he wanted to protect her but had neither the courage nor the ability to oppose the gringo. The atmosphere of tension was broken by the American's laughter.

'I'm not looking to cause trouble. I came here for something to eat and with the hope of finding some relax-ation.' He looked meaningfully at the girl. 'Here,' he produced a silver dollar from his pocket almost with the same rapidity as he'd earlier drawn his six-gun and flipped it in her direction, 'I'm sure you'll play me a tune in exchange for that.'

Without any attempt being made to capture it, the spinning coin hit the floor, rolled and rattled to a halt. Motionless, the girl sat and stared at the American. She struggled to keep her face expressionless, but the flare in her passionate eyes made it clear that she was insulted by the American's money.

'Pick it up,' the American told her. 'I'm sure it's not the first time you've been paid to entertain a man.'

The Mexican owner, finding confidence from the American's avowal that he wasn't seeking trouble, spoke up. 'She has only played to amuse herself,' he declared. 'No one has paid her.'

'A girl comes into a saloon alone for only one reason,' answered the American. 'Money. And she doesn't usually care how she earns it.' He glared at the girl, noted how she'd paled and how her hands had formed tight fists. 'So why don't you pick up the dollar and pluck out a tune on that instrument, because, by golly, before this night is over you're going to earn it one way or another.'

A slight tremor could be detected in her voice when she uttered her defiance. 'You wouldn't dare touch me.'

'No, *señor*.' The owner added his protest to the girl's, finding an unsuspected streak of courage. 'You must not.'

'Must not?' repeated the American.

'I will kill you if you touch me,' said the girl.

The American scoffed her words. 'Strong men have sworn to do that, yet I'm still here.'

'I will succeed,' she declared.

The American moved and spoke at the same time. 'Let's see,' he said, his words a challenge as his hands reached out and grabbed her upper arms. Pulling her to her feet he forced her backwards towards the bead curtain that separated the main room from the corridor that led to the bedrooms.

Taken by surprise and completely

overpowered by the American's strength, the girl was pushed backwards without being able to offer any real resistance. She tried to struggle but he held her upper arms so tightly that she was unable to use them to strike him on any part of his body, and when she tried to hamper him by not moving her legs he merely lifted her off the ground and carried her through to the bedroom.

Behind them, the consternation of the owner and his patrons raised little more than a murmur of protest at the girl's plight. If there had been a sheriff in San Miguel then he would have been summoned, but such small towns as this depended on the *Federales* for law enforcement. Their nearest outpost was more than thirty miles away at Piedras Negras and their patrols were few and irregular; no one really cared what happened to the poor Mexicans who worked the land.

The American crashed through the door of the first room off the corridor and pushed the girl away from him.

'I'll kill you,' she said, repeating her earlier threat, and instantly, from some fold in her skirt, she produced a long, thin-bladed knife which she gripped in a manner which would enable her to stab her attacker. She rushed forward, her arm upraised, her face contorted in an expression that confirmed her ability to deliver a deadly blow.

However, the American was prepared for it. He grasped her wrist and twisted. Involuntarily, the girl opened her hand and the knife fell to the floor. She cried out in frustration and tried to shake herself free from his grasp. He released his hold on her arms only to sweep her off the ground and throw her on to the bed.

'No,' she protested, but he was on top of her in a moment, his hands once more finding her wrists so that he could hold her arms outstretched from her body. Hopelessly, she struggled beneath him, hissing and cursing as his face came closer to her own.

He looked into the fire of her eyes

and knew at that moment that she hated him, but, as she twisted her head from side to side, his lips brushed against her ear and, urgently, he whispered, 'Inez Robles?'

The girl's reaction wasn't immediate; she continued for several moments to twist her head and body in an effort to avoid what she perceived to be the intention of the American, but slowly, just as the application of brakes by a coachman eventually brings his vehicle to a halt, so the fact that the American knew her name penetrated her mind. Her eyes opened wide, curiosity mingled with distrust.

'You are Inez Robles?' he asked.

She didn't speak but the cessation of her struggle told him he was correct. He dipped his head so that he could whisper his message into her ear:

'Your father is still alive.'

2

For an instant, hope and pleasure lit up the face of Inez Robles. Her mouth, which moments earlier had been grim and tight-lipped as it issued protests and oaths, now relaxed into its customary full-lipped shape, slightly open, thereby affording a glimpse of the white teeth within. Her eyes retained a bright gleam; no longer were they lit by the firebrand of her resolute defiance but were kindled by a beacon of elation. The tautness of her skin gave way to soft, full cheeks to which colour returned as though warmed by the same source as that which lit her eyes. The American's unexpected words swept from her mind all those dark thoughts with which it had been filled.

Above her, the American saw these changes and would not have been mortal if he hadn't been affected by them. Inez Robles had been described to him on more than one occasion but her brother's words had not done enough to prepare him for the effect that she had on him. All at once he realized the intimacy of the position in which he held her and rolled away. Swiftly he crossed to the door and pressed his ear to it.

Inez arose from the bed, her initial euphoria now replaced with a mind full of questions. Was it true that her father, whom she had last seen smothered in his own blood, was still alive? How did this stranger know what had happened to her father, or that she was his daughter? She had assumed that he was one of the gang who had attacked the *hacienda*, or a lone bandit who had come to San Miguel to escape the law on the far bank of the Rio Grande, but now she wasn't so sure. He had been rough and demanding under the observation of the men in the saloon but now that he had her attention his behaviour was different. Listening at the door was an act of caution but she detected no nervousness in his manner. He wasn't afraid of the men in the other room, just determined not to have their conversation overheard. He was tall, she noted, and strong, and she recalled how he'd lifted her off her feet without the slightest hesitation and carried her into this room. He was perhaps half a dozen years older than her brother but he acted with a maturity that was closer to her father's than to that of Luis. He made her nervous, but not afraid. Once more she adopted an expression of defiance and although it was mainly a reflection of her curiosity, it was still tinged with mistrust.

Satisfied that no one had followed them into the corridor the American returned to the girl. Without speaking, he held out his hand. In it was a gold signet ring, its face an oval of jet with the gold depiction of an eagle's head embedded in it.

'That belongs to my father,' she said.

'He told me to give it to you to prove that I'm acting on his behalf.'

'Who are you?' she asked.

'Dan Calloway.' Her reaction made it clear that the name was familiar to her. 'I came to Mexico to collect my horses,' he added.

'And my father?'

'He's alive. A doctor removed the bullet and probably saved his life but you must go home. You are needed there.'

She raised her chin an inch, rejecting the words she assumed were a criticism of her actions.

'I'm needed here, too. They have Luis. I mean to find him and bring him home.'

Dan Calloway bent down and picked up the dagger he'd wrenched from the girl's hand.

'Armed with this? It wasn't enough to defeat me so it hasn't got much hope against Dick Lazarus and his gang. They are ruthless. They won't show you any mercy.'

Dan Calloway could see that Inez Robles felt belittled by his words; if there had been a more gentle way of putting across his message he would have taken it, but the reputation of those who rode in the Lazarus gang denied him more courteous behaviour. He had to prevent the girl from pursuing the course she seemed determined to follow.

'Even if my father is alive, and I am grateful to God that he is, he is still unable to uphold the honour of our family. These men must not be allowed to get away with the attack they made on our home. It is my duty to seek for Luis,' she declared. 'There is no one else to do it.'

'I'll find Luis,' Dan told her.

'You! Why?'

'Your brother and I have been friends for several years. Besides, some of those horses they stole were mine. I mean to get back what belongs to me.'

'My family will replace your loss, Mr Calloway, or return your money.'

'It doesn't work that way, Miss Robles. With horses a deal is a deal. I paid my money so the horses are mine.'

A look of determination settled on the face of Inez Robles, making it clear that she would not be easily swayed from her mission to find her brother. Dan Calloway was equally determined that she should return home.

'Your father is alive,' he told her, 'but only just and your absence isn't helping his recovery. He's worried about you, can't rest properly because he knows you are in danger. Your mother begs you to return home and ease his mind.'

'And Luis?' she asked. 'Do I just forget my brother?'

Dan Calloway spoke bluntly to the girl, he knew there was nothing to be gained by treating her with gentleness or offering false hope; her family had survived in this place despite rebellions and border raiders, so she was aware of the fragility of life.

'If Luis is still alive then it is probable they will demand a ransom for his return. In that eventuality, and with your father incapacitated, you need to be at the hacienda to act on behalf of the family.'

The girl had known that a ransom demand was a probable outcome: other families had been attacked by the Lazarus gang and treated in similar fashion. Old Mexican families had been stripped of their most valuable possessions and their property rased. Even so, she was also aware that not every hostage had been returned, which was why she was determined to find her brother. It was known throughout the territory that the gang regularly used San Miguel as a base so, if Luis was still alive, she believed they would bring him here. By pretending to be a saloon singer she hoped to overhear unguarded conversations that would gain her sufficient information to rescue him. It was a simple plan but as Dan Calloway had pointed out, she hadn't the armaments to challenge them physically. Success depended on her guile and courage.

'They'll bring him here,' she said, her tone still implying that she wanted to remain, to be instrumental in his rescue.

Dan nodded his agreement; the information he'd gathered at the home of the Robles family had led him to the same conclusion.

'I'll remain here for two days. If they haven't come in that time then they aren't coming.' He paused to make sure the girl understood the implication of such an eventuality, that Luis was dead. 'After that, I'll cross the river and track down the horses. The gang is wanted by the law in Texas, too. When I find them I'll make sure they are made to pay for their crimes.'

'Two days,' she said, bargaining, 'then I'll return home.'

'No. It would kill your father if anything happened to you and your mother needs you, too. In the morning we'll find someone to accompany you back to the hacienda.'

'You don't dictate what I do,' she told him.

'It's your father's wish,' he told her, knowing the respect that the children of established Mexican families had for their parents. It was apparent to Dan Calloway that no matter how reluctant Inez was to quit San Miguel, she would be even more reluctant to disobey her father. 'Is there anyone in this town you can trust?' he asked.

'Pedro, the owner of this cantina. He worked for my father when I was a child. He knows me. He will find someone to escort me home.'

'Are you known by anyone else?'

'One or two, I suppose. I sometimes accompany my father when he comes here.'

This wasn't welcome information for Dan. The more people who knew Inez the more likely it was that her identity and presence in San Miguel would become known to Dick Lazarus if the gang was still in the vicinity. He also knew that if he returned to the barroom showing any kind of accord with the girl that too would be reported to the raiders.

'You'll have to spend the night with me in this room,' he announced. 'In the morning you can pretend I've used you badly, which will give you an excuse for leaving town.'

She cast a suspicious look at him, unsure for a moment how much of a danger he was to her.

'If they show up, I need to blow smoke in the eyes of our enemies,' he explained. 'It wouldn't help me if someone reported to the Lazarus gang that I'd been in the company of the sister of the man they were holding hostage. But if they think I abused you while we were together they are more likely to see me as a man of their own stripe. Just make a lot of noise about it when you leave.'

To add veracity to the scene he was attempting to construct, Dan opened the door and yelled for Pedro to bring a bottle of whiskey, but it was with a troubled mind that Inez Robles sat on the bed while they waited for the appearance of the rotund Mexican.

Although it had not been put into words she knew that she had acceded to the insistent American's demand that she quit San Miguel. While her desire to find her brother was not weakened by this change in her plans she was amazed by the thought that the hunt for him was now in more capable hands. Again, she found herself observing the big American in secretive fashion, as though an open gaze might reveal something that she didn't want him to see, or might pass a message to him that she didn't want to give.

Pedro knocked at the door, a tentative tap which Dan Calloway instantly answered. He beckoned the man into the room and closed the door. It was clear that whatever scene Pedro had expected to see inside the room, it was not the one before him. The American took the bottle from him and stood it on the dressing table behind the door. Inez Robles, composed and quiet, allowed a smile to relax her face. To the Mexican it seemed that the burden that had been settled upon her since she'd first arrived in town had been raised from her shoulders and, even though there was still a tautness about her movements, she looked more like the carefree girl he had known for almost twenty years.

'We need your help,' began Dan, and he outlined the need to get Inez back to her hacienda and the need to give the false impression that she had spent the night in his room against her will.

Pedro had a cousin, Rodolfo, who could be trusted to accompany Inez and who would be ready to ride early next morning. After assuring them that he would soon be closing the cantina for the night, he departed.

Dan Calloway told Inez to get some sleep but that was an instruction she had difficulty in obeying. He was, after all, a stranger and it wasn't her custom to be alone with a man in his bedroom. Her wariness was obvious, so Dan suggested that she told him about the raid on her home. So far he had learned only the bare bones of the raid. If he had to track the gang he needed to know more details about the individual members. He hoped that Inez could supply that information.

'It was late when they came,' she began. 'One of our outriders came to the hacienda to report that two or three rustlers were trying to drive off the cattle from the south range. My father ordered most of our crew to ride out and chase them away. Two or three men didn't seem like much of a threat and he suspected that they would flee at the appearance of a larger group.

'However, no sooner were our men out of sight than it became clear that the disturbance among the cattle had been a set-up, a decoy to draw the main force away from our home. A group of perhaps twenty men came from the north with the ambition of driving off our horses which were corralled near the house. Papa and Luis grabbed rifles and went out to defend our property. They were joined by the two men who had remained behind.'

She paused, picturing the scene that had unfolded. Horsemen carrying flaming firebrands had circled the horse enclosure in an attempt to stampede the beasts and drive them north away from the ranch and the workforce who had been tricked into riding south. Other men attacked the house, discharging guns and flinging their burning torches at the windows in order to create panic among those inside.

'When our men fought back they were ruthlessly shot down,' said Inez. 'My father was the first one shot. As soon as he left the house they opened fire and he fell. Luis, too, I believe, thought our father was dead. He went crazy, ran into the courtyard firing his rifle rapidly. He killed the man who had shot Papa, and two, perhaps three others. But his rifle was soon empty and I feared that he, too, would be killed. But a big man rode up and clubbed Luis with the butt of his rifle. Unconscious, he was slung over someone's saddle and then they all raced away in pursuit of the stolen horses.

'I went out with a rifle,' she continued, 'but they were out of range and in the darkness I don't suppose I would have hit anything, but I couldn't take the risk that a stray shot might hit Luis so I didn't pull the trigger. I attended to Papa. There was an awful hole in his chest and blood had saturated his shirt. I was sure he was dead. One of the other men was wounded and being tended by his friend.

'I found Mama fighting the small fires in the house with the cook and the maid. I told her what had happened to Papa and Luis. It occurred to me that Luis had been taken for a reason; it would have been easy for the raiders to kill him, too, but they hadn't. So I saddled up and began to seek their trail. I lost it, but knew that they often descended on San Miguel when they were hiding from the American lawmen. If they meant to ransom him it seemed a likely place to hold him.'

'But they haven't been here?'

She shook her head. 'Pedro has not seen them for several months.'

'Perhaps they've found a new place of sanctuary.'

Inez raised her eyes to his, her look told him that that was a possibility she'd considered but didn't want to believe. She'd convinced herself that if she caught up with them she could effect the rescue of her brother; if they didn't come to San Miguel then she knew not where to find them.

'All the more reason why you should be at home.' Dan Calloway's voice was soft. He'd already convinced her that chasing these men was not a job for her, so he had no more need to be rough with her. 'If they mean to contact you that is where they'll send their message.'

Her head dropped, her chin was almost touching her chest. Dan didn't want her to be dejected by the fact that she was going home; he was impressed by her bravery, few men would have pursued the Lazarus gang unless they were part of a posse.

'Perhaps you can still help me,' he said. 'I know nothing about these men except their reputation. Can you describe any of them? If I can recognize them before they know I'm hunting them it could give me a slight advantage.'

'It was dark when they came,' she said, 'but I think the big man, the one who clubbed Luis, was their leader. I saw his face briefly by the flame of one of the torches. The lower part was covered in stubble but there was definitely a long scar on his left cheek.'

'Anything else?'

'No, but the man who put Luis on the horse was wearing a grey uniform jacket and forage hat.'

'Confederate grey?'

'Yes,' she said. 'I have seen those jackets worn by other Americans on this side of the river.'

'Thank you,' said Dan, 'every bit of information helps me. Now,' he added, 'you need to lie down and get some sleep. It's a long ride home tomorrow.'

Inez put her head on the pillow and closed her eyes. Dan made himself comfortable in the chair near the window. From the bed the girl's voice carried to him.

'If they haven't shown after two days will you let me know?'

'Yes, Miss Robles, I'll let you know.' After a moment he added, 'If Luis can still be found I promise I'll bring him home.'

3

There weren't many people about next morning when Inez Robles quit the cantina, but those who were could later give testament to the fact that the girl had departed in a dishevelled and distressed manner. Their suspicions of the American's treatment of her were more or less confirmed by the string of vitriolic comments to which she gave voice as she stepped into the street.

In fact, her parting from Dan Calloway had been an event of embarrassed politeness. To the last moment she strove to find an argument that would keep her from returning home but his stern expression had made it clear that he would countenance no objections. Once more, she evoked a promise from him to keep her informed; then, deliberately ripping the bodice of her dress, she left him and began the masquerade for the half a dozen peons who were going about their business in the marketplace.

Dan Calloway didn't watch her performance from the window; he, too, needed to play his part and be the bullying American the townspeople of San Miguel believed him to be. Accordingly, he pretended no further interest in her though, in truth, he had been impressed by more than her courage. For several moments he dwelt on the memory of her face and especially those bright, passionate eyes that had flashed at one moment with an expression of murder and at another with joy because her father was still alive. Giving a promise to keep her informed of events had been no hardship because hers was a face he hoped to see again.

Shortly after her departure Dan called for Pedro to join him in his room.

'I understand the Lazarus gang haven't been here recently.'

'No, *señor*.'

'Do they have another place of refuge?'

Pedro shrugged as though it was a question to which he couldn't possibly know the answer, but Dan suspected that it was nothing more than a customary response to questions from Americans.

'Come on, Pedro. There must be rumours about where they go. It was rumours that brought me to San Miguel to find them, and those same rumours brought the *señorita* here.'

'Señorita Robles should not have come here.'

'We're in agreement there, Pedro, but the Lazarus gang have taken her brother and shot her father. Her instinct is to fight back.'

'*Si, señor*, but what could she have done if those men had been here? What can any of us do when they ride in? Nothing. We are farmers, *señor*, not fighters.'

'You could call in the *Federales*.

They would arrest them.'

Pedro's face twisted in a semi-smile, the humour, Dan suspected, was aimed at him, an outsider who had no grasp of the situation.

'They won't help?' Dan asked.

'Señor, they have their own priorities in these matters.'

'You mean they are being paid to look the other way?'

'It would not be safe for me to say that,' Pedro told Dan, 'but no one can remember when the soldiers last came to San Miguel.'

Dan rubbed his chin as he thought. Eventually he said, 'Why did you say Señorita Robles should not have come here? What danger is there if the Lazarus gang aren't going to show up?'

'The gang has several friends in this town, men who pass on information and who ride herd on rustled cattle.'

'Would they recognize the señorita?'

'Si, señor, most people know the Robles family.'

'And has news of the attack on their

hacienda reached San Miguel?'

It had; a carter had brought the news the previous day and it had spread around the town like wildfire. As a consequence, people had begun to speculate on the peculiar presence of Inez Robles in San Miguel. No one guessed that her intention was to wage war on the gang but, nonetheless, her often silent visits to the cantina had brought about an oppressive atmosphere, which caused most people to fear for the girl's safety.

'Those who were here last night believe that you are one of the gang, that you came to discourage her from following whatever plan she had,' Pedro told Dan.

'Which means that someone would have reported her behaviour?'

Pedro gave one of his shrugs.

'Do you know who?' asked Dan.

The answer was another shrug.

'Come on, Pedro, you know everything that goes on in this town. Who has been absent for a day and where did they go?'

Pedro was reluctant to talk; giving

information to Americans about his own people didn't sit easily with him. Dan had been an outsider in a community many times and he recognized the silence for the discretion that it was.

'I understand the Robles family are your friends; well, they are mine, too. Telling me what you know will help them and hopefully will lead to Luis's freedom.'

'You know the Robles family? Truly?'

'Luis and I have been friends for several years, but if I'm to get him away from the Lazarus gang I'm going to need all the help I can get. Where is he, Pedro? Who in this town would inform that the sister of their prisoner was waiting in San Miguel?'

Pedro didn't answer instantly. As Dan himself had done the previous night, he went to the door, opened it and checked the corridor to make sure they weren't being overheard.

'There is a man called Rodrigo Suarez who has done much business with the gang. He has bought cattle they've brought from the other side of the Rio Grande and sold it at the Monterrey meat markets. He has a brother, Hernandez, who has ridden with the gang. They were here when the *señorita* arrived but were not around the next day. Perhaps they can give you the information you are seeking.'

'Where will I find them?'

'Rodrigo has a little farm north of here. When they aren't sleeping in the sun in the marketplace they can be found sleeping in the sun out there.'

Furnished with directions for finding the farm, Dan Calloway quit the cantina and went in search of his horse which Pedro had corralled the previous night when it had become obvious that he wouldn't be needed before morning. The trail to the north of San Miguel was a long, sweeping arc that followed the natural contours of the dry, brush-covered ground. This was the tail end of the Chihuahuan Desert, yet men had gathered great herds of cattle in this terrain just as their American counterparts had done in similar conditions on the far bank of the Rio Grande. Crops, too, had been raised, primarily cotton, but the peons had scratched and watered small portions of land on which they grew sufficient food for their families.

Dan Calloway admired those men. His own ranch was many miles to the north, in Nebraska, in the luxuriant pasture land close to the confluence of the north and south streams that formed the Platte. As with all terrains, Dan reflected, it had its challenges, but nothing in comparison with relentless battle that had to be waged in this sparse, sunbaked territory. Yet they reared horses fine enough to bring him across hundreds of miles of dangerous country. Was that, he wondered, a mark of Señor Robles's talent or the quality of the animal's breed, which had originated hundreds of years ago in Europe.

In the unfamiliar land, he seldom

pricked the horse to travel at more than a canter. Huge boulders that had been carried and deserted by the great transformations of the planet presented both obstacles and landmarks for his journey. Arroyos of varying depths appeared suddenly and required negotiating. Sometimes, when he could follow them without changing his direction, he descended to the beds of these channels in order to take advantage of the shade they offered. But always he kept an eye on the trajectory of the sun, reassuring himself that he hadn't strayed from his route. Every now and then he saw one of the landmarks that Pedro had told him to watch out for, and when he reached the thin stream that straggled in an easterly direction he knew he was close to the farm that belonged to the Suarez brothers.

From the cover of some nearby boulders Dan observed the farm. A handful of unattractive hens scraped about in the yard at the side of the house, fluttering here and there whenever they sensed a worm or an insect that would satisfy their hunger. Dan knew they were hungry because they were so thin that they didn't seem worth killing for the mean meal they would provide. A couple of goats, tethered to short posts, were bleating as they tried to find grass in a yard they had already picked clean. A small corral was empty of animals and a dilapidated barn whose roof sagged due to the loss of several timber slats was empty too. Dan knew this because its doors stood open, as though someone had left hurriedly with little intention of returning.

The farmhouse was an adobe building of larger proportions than Dan had expected. It was a single-storey, flat-roofed construction with a surrounding parapet. Below that, a wooden portico provided shade at the door and the deep-set windows probably kept the interior cool. It had been a fine home but now the once white walls were chipped and grey and any paint that had once coloured the timbers had long since been stripped away by heat and wind-whipped sand. There was an unused hitching pole in front of the house and a long water trough across the yard.

The possibility that he was in the wrong place occurred briefly to Dan but he soon dismissed it; he had been guided by Pedro's landmarks and not missed one. Pedro had also spoken of the laziness of the brothers and Dan wondered if they were asleep inside the house. Again, it was another thought quickly put aside. The place, he was sure, was deserted, it wore an atmosphere of neglect, but he couldn't tell if that was permanent.

Frustrated by the absence of the Suarez brothers, Dan decided that his only course of action was to ride down to the farm and take a look around. His expectation of finding a clue to the location of the Lazarus gang was low and it would be difficult to explain his presence on the property if he was caught there, but he had always known that any hope he had of rescuing Luis would involve risk and prompt action.

Before he could act, however, the sound of galloping horses reached him and he withdrew once more among the rocks where he could secretly observe the farm house below.

Within a minute he heard whip cracks and the yells of a man driving his team to their best exertion. Moments later the vehicle came into view. Two horses, manes and tails flying as they raced along the trail were pulling a black, yellow-wheeled buggy which bounced and swayed as it touched each rut in the road. It bore two men, and tied to the back were three horses. Each man was wearing dark clothing and a flat-topped sombrero. Even though sitting it was clear to Dan that they were lanky, certainly taller than most Mexican men he'd encountered, and there was something in their bearing, as though coiled in anticipation of a sudden attack that suggested they were members of the same family. He had little doubt that he was witnessing the return home of the Suarez brothers.

The driver pulled harshly on the reins as they reached the adobe house and his companion jumped to the ground. In the area behind the front seat there was a large bundle which would have escaped Dan's notice if the man who had disembarked had not prodded at it in savage fashion. Dan thought his intention must be to unload it but he didn't, moving instead to the rear of the buggy where he untied the trailing horses and hitched them to the nearby rail. With words and gesticulations he urged his brother to drive on while he went into the house.

The buggy was driven fully into the barn where, occasionally, from his vantage point, Dan caught glimpses of the driver as he went about the task of unharnessing the team from the vehicle. A few minutes later, he watched as the lanky Mexican quit the barn, closed the doors and went into the house. Now he decided to ride down to the farm and learn what he could from the Suarez brothers.

They had seen him, or heard the sound of his horse's hoof beats before he was within a hundred yards of the house. Both men stepped outside and watched his slow approach from the shade of the listing wooden portico. With their dark apparel and dark skin, Dan knew that their movements would be difficult to see if this confrontation turned to violence. Already, their stance warned him that he was unwelcome; each man had his right hand close to a holstered weapon, and by the way the guns were worn low on the thigh Dan knew that they were not reluctant to use them. He pulled to a halt a dozen strides from the house.

'Hot day,' he said, removing his hat and wiping his brow to add emphasis to his words. The brothers remained silent, scrutinizing their visitor through narrowed eyes, almost as though they were waiting for a sign that would define Dan as a friend or an enemy.

'I could use a drink of water,' said the American.'

The answer from the shadows came in a low, threatening voice: '*Non comprende.*'

Dan realized that they were going to plead an ignorance of English, but that, he calculated, was unlikely. Pedro had told him that one of the brothers had ridden with the Lazarus gang: it was impossible to believe that he hadn't picked up enough English to understand his request. However, using one of the few Spanish words he knew, he tried once more.

'*Agua,*' he said and raised his hand to his mouth to demonstrate his need.

One of the brothers stepped forward and pointed to his left.

'Rio Bravo,' he growled, using the Mexican name for the Rio Grande, making it clear that Dan would not receive any hospitality at this place. To make sure that Dan got the message his hand settled on the butt of his revolver and his eyes fixed on the American in an unfriendly stare.

Dan had little doubt that the visit of

an American to their farm was a rare event, but the previous night the townspeople of San Miguel had believed him to be one of the Lazarus gang so perhaps he could pass himself off in that guise here. But the unflinching gaze of the man before him made that seem unlikely. If, as Pedro had hinted, they had reported Inez Robles to the gang then they would know that he wasn't one of that group. In those circumstances they would assume he was a lawman and would probably shoot him.

He wasn't slow with a gun but at the moment they had a distinct advantage: he'd ridden in peacefully, kept his hands on his saddle horn to show that he wasn't a threat, but they had their hands on their guns and would shoot him out of the saddle the moment he made any threatening move. Being dead wouldn't get him back his horses or Luis Robles. He tipped his hat and rode away, wondering what he could do to get information from them.

He rode off towards the Rio Bravo

but when he was beyond sight of the farmhouse he circled back so that he could retake the vantage point he'd occupied earlier. A quick scan of the farm revealed that the barn doors were open and after a few moments both brothers emerged and headed for the house. They stopped in the yard, deep in conversation, then one of them unhitched one of the horses and climbed into the saddle. His brother continued talking and although his voice didn't carry to Dan it seemed clear by his gestures that he was issuing instructions. A final exchange of words, then the rider tapped his steed's flanks and it was running at speed away from the little farm.

For a moment Dan was unsure what course of action to take. He could either follow the rider in the hope that he would lead him to the location of the Lazarus gang or attempt to take the remaining brother by surprise and force some answers from him. Because his priority was to find Luis Robles and the horses, he chose the former. The horseman was heading in his direction but suddenly swung to the east and quickly moved out of sight. Dan mounted and set off in pursuit.

Fortunately, the trail was easy to follow. Hoofprints showed clearly in the loose, sandy ground, an advantage to Dan, who could allow his quarry to stay far enough ahead so that he would never know he was being followed. Dan prayed he had made the right decision and that he was being led to the place where Luis was held captive.

There was no board bearing the name of the place he arrived at forty minutes later. It was doubtful if the small collection of buildings appeared on any map. The only thing it had in common with San Miguel was that a well marked its centre. This access to water was probably the sole reason for the settlement. Dan drew rein in the shade of the first building and dismounted.

A woman in a black dress and shawl

was raising water at the well. She turned her head as he approached, startled by his sudden appearance and alarmed by the expression on his face. When he reached her he scooped a handful of water from the raised bucket and swilled his face.

'*Gracias*,' he said, but he wasn't looking at her, his eyes were fixed on the sweating horse that was hitched outside one of the small adobe buildings. Only one other horse was tethered there, which quashed any hope Dan had that this place was the new refuge of Dick Lazarus and his men. The Suarez brother's reason for being here could be entirely innocent, perhaps he visited a woman at that house. The only way Dan would find out would be by crossing the space between. He lifted the gun in his holster, ensuring it would come out without snagging if he needed it, then began walking towards the building he had targeted. Behind him the woman crossed herself as though she was in the presence of the Devil, but she made no other movement and remained silent.

Walking with a determined stride, Dan covered half the distance; then, noting that his shadow stretched out before him, he veered to his right so that it wouldn't fall through the open door and warn those inside of his approach. Cautiously, edging silently along the wall, he got nearer to the door. When he could hear the low murmur of voices, he paused. A quick scan of the street told him that he had not attracted the attention of anyone except the woman at the well. She stood as still as a statue, with the heavy bucket in her right hand. Like that of a widow at a funeral, the black shawl that had covered her shoulders was now draped over her head and wrapped around the lower portion of her face. For a moment they watched each other, then the spell was broken when words, uttered in a heavy Mexican accent, reached Dan.

'Tell Lazarus we have the prisoner

secure at our farm, tell him to demand a lot of money. I know the Robles family, they are too proud not to pay a ransom.'

Dan Calloway digested that information. Luis Robles, it seemed was being held at the farm he'd had under observation and he had a feeling that he had had a quick glimpse of his friend without realizing it at the time. The bundle in the back of the buggy, which had been ferociously prodded by one of the brothers, had, he believed, been Luis Robles. That knowledge was all the encouragement he needed to step through the doorway.

It was a small, dim room, ill-designed so that sunlight failed to reach a large portion of it. There were two occupants; Suarez, the speaker, and an overweight American whose face, wet with sweat, was grimy and unshaven. They faced each other across a crude table and both turned towards the door when Dan kicked it further open.

'Your English has improved,' Dan

said. 'If you'd told me about your prisoner when I was at your home it would have saved me a tiring journey.'

'The gringo,' said Suarez, his voice loud and angry. 'I knew he was a lawman.'

Instantly his right hand dropped beneath the level of the table, grasping for the handle of his revolver. His chair tumbled away behind him as he began to rise to his feet, striving to give himself more freedom to draw his weapon. It was a foolish move. Dan's only disadvantage in the situation was that he was lit up by the brilliant daylight, but everything happened so quickly that that hardly mattered. Dan drew and shot before Suarez had cleared his holster. The Mexican yelled as the bullet tore into his body and threw him backwards on to the floor, where he lay very still.

Dan swung his arm so that his gun was pointed at the fat American's belly. The man had barely moved since Dan had stepped into the room and he knew that it was too late now to offer resistance. He raised his hands above his shoulders, eyes bulging, desperately hoping that the newcomer would be less ruthless than he would be if the situation was reversed.

'We were just talking,' he blurted out. 'I have no argument with you.'

'Do you ride with Dick Lazarus?'

The man licked his lips, preparing to lie, but Dan had already proved his ability with a revolver and the steadiness with which it was now pointed at the fat man's body convinced him that this was not a time for anything but total submission. He nodded.

'Did you take part in the raid on the hacienda of Don Robles?'

Again, the fat American answered with a nod of the head.

'Where is Dick Lazarus?' asked Dan, then, knowing though not understanding why Luis was being held at the farm of the Suarez brothers, he added, 'and where are the horses?'

'Across the Rio Grande,' the man replied. 'They are all in Texas now.'

It was the answer that Dan didn't want. If they'd still been in Mexico then it was probable that they weren't far away. That would have given him the opportunity to track them and recover his property, but once across the Rio Grande they could have ridden a trail in any direction, and until another outrage was reported he would never know where they were.

For a moment he considered what to do with his prisoner. There were no law officers in San Miguel, so it was impossible to conceive of any facility for detaining this man in this small village. Dan's first priority was to rescue Luis from the Suarez farm; he would be handicapping himself if he chose to take this man with him without any idea of where to find the nearest jail. It was a risk he wasn't prepared to take. He ordered the man to leave his gun on the table, then signalled for him to go into the street.

'Go,' he said. 'Don't let me see you again.'

With greater alacrity than would have been expected from a man of his size, the outlaw climbed on to his horse and rode away swiftly. Dan watched until he was so far away that it was clear he would not stop until he reached the border. Then Dan went to collect his horse.

In the bright sunshine the woman still stood near the well. Apart from the disturbance of her skirt by a slight breeze she was motionless. She watched the men emerge from the building and wondered what had happened to Hernandez Suarez, whom she had seen enter only minutes earlier. The gunshot had suggested an answer to that question but she was waiting for confirmation.

'Suarez,' she said, 'is he dead?'

'He's dead.'

'Did you kill him?'

'I killed him.'

'You should have killed that one, too. He's a bad man.'

4

It was well into the afternoon when Dan once more occupied the place among the group of boulders that gave him a commanding view of the Suarez farm. Nothing had changed since he had last stood on that spot. Two horses remained saddled and dozy in front of the house while the same weary goats in the side yard watched the dispirited antics of the hens as they continued a languid worm-hunt.

Dan assumed that the barn was still being used as a prison for Luis Robles. Its doors were open and he could see the high back of the buggy inside. The last time he'd ridden down to the farm the Suarez brothers had been aware of him before he was halfway to their door. This time he intended a more covert approach. He had already killed one brother; he didn't want to kill the other one unnecessarily.

After a quick scan of the surrounding terrain a plan soon formed in the American's mind. If he made a big enough detour, by using the available cover of boulders and trees he could reach the stream which ran around the back of the property. He had no idea of the layout of the house or of which areas of the surrounding land were overlooked by windows, but once he got into the stream, if he kept his head below the level of the bank he believed he would avoid detection. There was a sharp bend in the stream, from which point it was obscured from the house by the barn. Once out of the water, Dan could approach the barn from the rear.

Swiftly finding a suitable spot, he tethered his mount among the boulders, then prepared to set off on his rescue bid. A last glance towards the farm caused him to delay a little. Suarez was standing in the doorway of the house, scanning the horizon in

Dan's direction. Dan remained still, wondering if he had already betrayed his presence by some inadvertent movement. The more he watched, however, the more he believed that the Mexican's surveillance was of a more general nature than specific to the area in which he was hidden. It occurred to Dan that the man was watching for the return of his brother.

Dan watched while the man hovered in the doorway. Once or twice he took a step or two towards the barn but each time it was followed by another scan of the horizon, which halted his advance. To Dan, Suarez appeared to be a man on a short rein, someone struggling to suppress an overwhelming desire; anxious to go to the barn but wary of being caught there by his brother. Dan had no way of knowing the cause of the Mexican's extreme uneasiness but he didn't want to risk advancing until the other had quit his post at the front of the house. Suarez had lit a cheroot and was leaning over the rail to which the horses were tethered, still throwing occasional glances in the direction of the barn.

Eventually, with the cheroot only half-smoked, he ground the remainder under foot and went back into the house. Immediately, Dan was on the move. There was only one portion of the route he'd chosen that lacked natural cover but the house was quarter of a mile distant and the probability of being seen was low. Nonetheless, Dan crawled and rolled across the hard ground until he dropped over the lip of the gulch and into the swill of water, which was barely deep enough to cover the rock-strewn bed.

From there his progress was swift. He followed the water course in a stooped run until he'd negotiated the bend; then, hidden from the house, he made a dash to the back of the barn. Pausing long enough to ensure that the remaining Suarez brother had not re-emerged from the house, he edged his way cautiously along the side of the building, then darted through the open front door, confident that he had escaped observation.

Although the doors were open, the buggy, parked near the entrance, prevented the barn from being flooded with light, so it needed a few seconds for Dan's sight to adjust to the darkness. He stood motionless, leaning for a moment against one of the vehicle's high yellow wheels. He reached into the space behind the driver's seat but the bundle that he had seen there earlier was now gone. Deeper into the barn, something moved. Instinctively, Dan's hand dropped to the butt of his revolver, but he relaxed when he recognized the iron scrape of a shod hoof. Dan was cheered by the presence of horses. Luis would need one for the journey home.

'Luis,' he called, keeping his voice low in the hope that his friend would follow his lead. If they didn't alert the man in the house they might be halfway back to the hacienda before the escape was discovered.

It took a second hushed call before a shuffling and a low grunt reached his ears. He moved further into the stable, carefully, because the darkness was greater there.

'Luis,' he said again, and the responding sound seemed to be almost at his feet. He knelt and searched around with his hands. Almost immediately he made contact with a bundle wrapped in a coarse material, not unlike a blanket from under the saddle of a horse, and he was satisfied that it was a human form under his hands.

'Luis,' he said, 'it's Dan Calloway. Don't make too much noise and I'll soon have you out of here.'

The response was, again, a stifled grunt and Dan knew that under the blanket his friend was gagged as well as tied. He was searching his pocket for a clasp knife when the a noise outside the door made him aware that he had company.

Back-lit by the bright sunshine, Rodrigo Suarez was a silhouette in the frame of the doorway. He fired a few words towards the point where Dan was crouched, but in Spanish which Dan wasn't able to interpret. However, if Suarez had seen Dan enter the barn and the words had been addressed to him, there was little doubt that they were not words of welcome. Even though his voice was low the cruelty of his meaning carried clearly to the American. For a moment he remained silhouetted in the doorway; then, to Dan's surprise, as he stepped forward he began to unbuckle his gun-belt.

Dan Calloway couldn't fathom the Mexican's intention but he didn't waste too much time in thought. He launched himself forward, colliding with the man, hitting him in the chest with his shoulder and carrying him back towards the open door. Grappling together they tumbled out into the sunshine, the Mexican uttering oaths as he staggered and fell under the unexpected onslaught. Dan threw a punch which caught his opponent behind the ear and did little damage; then, as they struggled on the ground, he made an ineffectual attempt to knee Suarez in the groin.

The rangy Mexican wasn't a stranger to this kind of brawl and fought back instinctively. Although caught offguard, his wiriness made it difficult for any man to get an advantage over him. He twisted out of Dan Calloway's grasp and, having evaded the first two attempts to hurt him, made a strike of his own. He used his bony elbow to attack Dan's throat, aiming a blow which, if it had hit the spot intended, would have instantly incapacitated the American and ended the fight. Fortunately, Dan jerked his head aside at the last moment and the point of Rodrigo's bent arm connected with the side of Dan's neck rather than his throat. Even so, the pain inflicted was severe and Dan realized that he had underestimated the ability of his opponent.

Fighting for his life, Dan slung a punch, careless of it finding its mark, its purpose being to deter Suarez from making another attempt at his throat. The punch connected and once again it was high on the Mexican's head. This time, however, it had a more telling effect, dislodging him from the advantageous position of being astride Dan's chest and Dan completed the separation by pushing him clear.

On his knees, Dan renewed his attack, stretching forward to deliver a punch at the prostrate Mexican, but as he inched closer, his opponent turned suddenly and threw a handful of dust and small stones into his face. Dan's punch lost its ferocity and while he wiped the particles away from his eyes, Suarez jumped to his feet and unleashed a kick at Dan's chest. The wind was driven from his body and he rolled across the ground, aware that another kick was imminent. Instinctively, he coiled into the foetal position, offering the smallest target possible. He took the next kick on his arms, then, in a change of tactics, reversed the direction of his roll so that he crashed into the Mexican.

In getting close to Suarez, Dan's purpose had been to reduce the power he'd be able to generate into his next kick. Luck was with him and he achieved more than that. At the point of impact, Suarez had been standing on his left leg, the right one drawn back, midway through the execution of another strike. Suarez stumbled as Dan collided with his supporting leg; by the time he'd regained his balance Dan had risen to his feet.

In the moment that they faced each other, recognition of his opponent showed on the Mexican's face. Again he spoke in Spanish but the only words Dan recognized were gringo and Hernandez and guessed that Rodrigo was reiterating his brother's belief that he was a lawman. But there was little time for conjecture. A long-bladed knife appeared suddenly in Rodrigo's hand, the expression on his face matched the deadliness of the weapon. He lunged so swiftly that the possibility of drawing his revolver got no further than being a thought in Dan's head.

Dan smacked away the first swipe, then gripped the Mexican's wrist as he brought the blade back in a reverse arc. Dan forced the arm high, his left hand holding the other's knife hand at the wrist while his right fended off a jab from the other's left fist. Each man tried to gain advantage by wrapping a leg behind those of his opponent and pushing him to the ground. First one then the other seemed likely to succeed, but eventually Dan's superior strength put an end to Rodrigo's elusive twisting and scheming and with a mighty heave he threw him over his outstretched leg. At the same time, he jerked the Mexican's wrist so that the knife spun away and landed some distance behind Dan.

Rodrigo was down but not out. Almost instantly he sprang to his feet and began running towards the house. Dan called for him to halt but the Mexican merely cast a glance over his shoulder and kept going. If Dan had believed that his opponent was quitting the fray he'd have been content to let him go, but Suarez had fought like a man who would be reluctant to surrender. And so it proved.

When he reached the tethered horses he stepped between them, keeping low so that little of his body could be seen. Dan knew his intention but, agile as his brain was, Suarez acted without hesitation. He drew a rifle from a boot attached to one of the animals and fired over that beast's back. Dan threw himself to his right and rolled a few more yards, with bullets hacking the ground in his wake. His sanctuary was the water trough, behind which he breathed deeply and drew his gun. For the moment he couldn't get a clear shot at his enemy but he now knew that the fight would surely end in the death of one of them.

He squirmed along the ground to the far end of the trough and peered round the side. A bullet smashed into the ground near his head; he swiftly withdrew to safety, but he had confirmed that Suarez was still between the horses, using them as a shield. A bullet thudded into the thick wooden trough as Dan attempted another reconnaissance; this time he did not withdraw. Instead he fired his pistol, twice, not aiming at Suarez but to the rear of the nearest horse. The bullets zipped past, so close that they almost disturbed its tail, causing it to swing its rear end, which crashed into the Mexican and squeezed him against the other animal.

Suarez lost control of his rifle, almost dropped it but was himself knocked to the ground when Dan further spooked the horse with another shot close to its rump. When Dan saw the man on the ground he rolled away from the water trough and fired two more shots under the horse. Both found their target and, with a final fling of his arms, Rodrigo Suarez died on the hard ground in front of his house.

Dan Calloway looked down at the body. It was only now that he realized how much alike the brothers had been; he wondered if they had been twins. It was a matter of no significance to him, they were dead and his friend could now be returned to his home. On his way to the barn he picked up the knife that Suarez had planned to use on him. With it he began to cut through the robes that secured the blanket-covered prisoner.

'It's Dan, Luis,' he said as he severed the bonds. 'Time to get out of here.' As the last binding parted and he pulled away the blanket he recoiled with surprise. The gagged prisoner was not Luis Robles. It was his sister, Inez.

5

Several moments passed before words were exchanged, during which, at the earliest opportunity, Inez Robles spat the gag from her mouth in order to fill her lungs with great inhalations. As soon as the retaining ropes were severed she spread, stretched and rubbed her arms and legs, which had been restrained from independent movement for several hours. After an initial wide-eyed glance at Dan Calloway, a look that described her anxiety with more clarity than words could have achieved, she endeavoured to keep her face from him while she tended to the task of exciting the circulation of blood through her body.

So unexpected had the girl's appearance been to the American that he had taken a backward step, as though needing to view the figure from a different perspective in order to convince his mind that his eyes weren't lying. Then the look she had thrown in his direction, which so well defined her vulnerability, took his thoughts off on a disagreeable tangent. He recalled the behaviour of Rodrigo Suarez as he'd watched from the cover of the boulders above the farm. It was clear that a battle had been raging inside the Mexican and now the cause of that conflict was clear. The prisoner in the barn was at his mercy and his instincts were urging him to take advantage of the girl before his brother returned. Eventually, those instincts had won, albeit too late to be satisfied.

Yet Dan couldn't rid himself of the memory of the look in the girl's eye and he wondered what harm she'd already been subjected to.

'Inez,' he said, concern for her well-being making him forget to address her in the formal style that was appropriate to the daughter of a man of her father's heritage, 'did they hurt you?'

She lifted her head to him and looked him in the eyes.

'No,' she said.

Her answer was given so quickly that Dan wasn't sure that she was telling the truth, but he knew that this wasn't a moment to argue with her. His eyes scanned her face and her clothing. Somewhere along the trail after leaving San Miguel she'd discarded the saloon-like dress she'd been wearing in favour of dark jeans and a bright yellow shirt. There was nothing to suggest mistreatment, so he took her at her word and asked how she had become the prisoner of the Suarez brothers.

She and Rodolfo, Pedro's cousin, had been accosted a few miles from San Miguel and it had been apparent that the brothers had been waiting for them. Inez surmised that they had watched them leave town, then had ridden hard to reach a suitable place to spring their ambush. Rodolfo had been shot, killed, Inez supposed although she had been too busy struggling with her attackers to know his fate for certain. They had gagged her, tied her and brought her to their farm in all haste.

'Did you recognize them?'

'Of course,' she replied. 'They are the worst of men. In the past they have stolen from our herd but they have always got rid of the stock before being caught. My father never had the proof to prosecute them. I suppose they intended to hold me for ransom, then quit this territory for good.'

'They intended handing you over to Dick Lazarus.' He indicated the body lying in the yard. 'I overheard his brother discussing their plan with one of the Lazarus gang. I thought they were talking about Luis.'

Inez got to her feet but she needed Dan's support to walk outside. Although the sunlight and clean air were instantly beneficial, she still clung to the big American's arm for several moments.

'We should go before Hernandez returns,' she said.

'Hernandez isn't coming back,' he

told her, his tone making his meaning unmistakable.

The expression on the girl's face remained unaltered. The revelation that her captors were dead induced neither pleasure nor sorrow.

'I haven't thanked you for rescuing me,' she said.

'That's unnecessary,' he told her, 'but you are right that we need to leave this place.' He examined her visually again and once more was warmed by her character. That look of determination had returned to her face, consigning her captivity to the back reaches of her mind. Still, he considered it probable that, following that ordeal, she needed a few minutes alone.

'My horse is tethered up there,' he told her, pointing to the boulders some distance from the farm. 'You can wash down at the stream while I go for him. Then we'll consider how best to get you back to the hacienda.'

He gave her fifteen minutes, during which time he tried to sort out the quandary in which he found himself. He had two tasks with equal priority. The Lazarus gang had crossed the river into Texas and their trail would soon be too cold to follow. If he hoped to catch them, recover his horses and rescue Luis Robles he couldn't delay matters for a moment. But it was equally important to get the girl back to her family, and that meant going in the opposite direction.

He collected the horses that were hitched to the front rail and led them down to the stream. Inez had not only rubbed from her face the scuff marks of bondage, but had added another article to her attire. The gun-belt that Rodrigo Suarez had removed when entering the barn was now snug around the girl's waist. Dan let it pass without comment. Seeing the horses, Inez identified the palomino as her own and climbed on to him in a moment.

'Do you know any nearby families?' he asked when they were ready to move out. Although he was reluctant to do so, considering the disaster the last attempt to get her home had turned into, his only chance of an early start in pursuit of the Lazarus gang was to entrust her into the care of someone who could be relied upon to protect her.

'Why?' she asked.

'I don't think it's safe for you in San Miguel. It would be better to leave you with people you know and trust.'

'That won't be necessary.'

'Miss Robles,' he said firmly, 'you can't ride home alone.'

'Why not?' she asked. 'I rode to San Miguel alone.'

Dan nodded his agreement but things were different now. No one had expected her to do what she'd done then, but now she could be prey to every lowlife who was seeking to gain favour with Dick Lazarus.

'Besides,' the girl added, 'I'm not going home. I'm going with you.' Dan was startled by the girl's declaration. 'You're going after the Lazarus gang, aren't you? Well I'm going, too.'

'You can't do that,' he said.

'Why not?'

'Because all I know is that they've crossed the river. They are in Texas and it could take me days, even weeks to locate them. And when I do I suppose people will die. I can't let that happen to you.'

'Are you going to kill men because they stole your horses?'

'Partly,' he said, 'but mainly because they've taken my friend.'

'Your friend is my brother. If you're prepared to kill to save him then so am I. In any case,' she added, 'if you leave me here I'll just follow you.'

'Then I'll take you home first.'

A touch of a smile spread over her lips; she knew she held the trump card.

'You can't do that, you would lose at least two days and any hope of finding your horses.'

'The horses aren't as important as your safety.'

'And my brother? You will sacrifice him in order to get me home?'

'I think that is what he would want me to do. Besides, someone needs to be at the hacienda to act upon any ransom demand.'

'My father, my mother, or our ranch overseer can do what needs to be done, but Lazarus will only be made to pay for his crimes by an unexpected strike against him. You and I, Mr Calloway, together we will surprise him and rescue Luis.'

'It's not right,' Dan Calloway said lamely. 'Days and weeks together, going who knows where. What will your father say?'

'I expect he'll make you marry me,' said Inez Robles, and the teasing smile that accompanied those words did little to make Dan enjoy the joke. She had understood his dilemma, her safety or the rescue of her brother, and had taken advantage of it.

★　★　★

They had been riding for half an hour before Inez asked where they were going.

'The Rio Bravo is over there,' she said, pointing to her left. 'That is the way to Texas.'

'Yes, I know, but perhaps this short detour will provide us with some information.'

Shortly after this they arrived at the place where Dan had killed Hernandez Suarez. Siesta hour had long since passed but a group of three men squatted in the shadow of an isolated building facing the well. From beneath their large hats their eyes followed the progress of the newcomers to their village. Dan stopped at the well, dismounted and allowed his horse to drink water from his hat. Inez copied his example.

Dan surveyed the dusty, sleepy place and wondered where the body of Hernandez Suarez had been taken. Perhaps, he mused, it had already been buried or perhaps dumped outside the village to be devoured by a wild cat or coyote. He glanced across at the men in the shade, who still kept their curiosity under their hats. Dan turned half a circle so that he was facing the building in which he'd confronted Hernandez Suarez. The door was closed and Dan wondered who the building now housed. No one else had been present during his earlier visit but he knew it wasn't the permanent abode of either Suarez or the American he'd chased back across the border.

'Wait here,' he told Inez Robles, then began to cross the sunbaked ground to the small adobe building. Halfway there, a movement to his right caught his attention. He half-turned, his right hand dropping defensively in the direction of his pistol butt. When he recognized the woman he'd spoken to earlier, he relaxed. She had emerged from the space between two houses, but the darkness of her clothes against the white-walled building gave her appearance a spectral quality, as though she was a shadow with depth, a three-dimensional apparition. Yet there was something so deliberate in her movement that Dan knew her purpose had been to attract his attention. He stopped, waited for her to approach.

'You've returned,' she said.

'I need information,' he told her. The woman looked over his shoulder. When Dan turned his head slightly he saw that Inez had followed him and stood close behind. 'I'm looking for Dick Lazarus. Does he come here?'

'You should go,' she said. 'Lazarus will kill you if he returns here.'

'When was his last visit?'

She didn't answer, her face maintained a stern expression as though she would answer no more questions.

'Who lives in that house?' Dan indicated the building that had been his destination before she'd intercepted him.

'I don't know,' she told him, which was an obvious lie.

Dan stepped forward but the woman placed herself between him and the door.

'It is empty,' she said.

This second lie was swiftly exposed. At that moment the door opened and an old woman called in a low, anxious voice, 'Rosina, Rosina.'

The woman who had detained Dan hurried towards the caller and in a torrent of Spanish words they disappeared inside the building.

'What was that about?' Dan asked Inez.

'Someone inside is ill.'

Without another word and with the girl in his wake, Dan followed the women into the house. Although it was empty, the room where Hernandez Suarez had died seemed smaller, but at the back, a door which had not been obvious on his first visit now stood open and female voices could be heard in the room beyond. In three strides Dan reached that door and looked inside the room.

The women were on either side of a low bed on which a youth lay. Bathed in sweat, his face was contorted with expressions of pain. The woman to whom Dan had spoken was attempting to cool his temperature by applying a damp cloth to his forehead. A bowl of water was set on a table at her side. Fear etched her face when she turned and saw Dan in the doorway.

'What ails him?' asked Dan.

'A fever.'

'Who is he?'

'My son.' The woman's softly spoken words were a mixture of defiance and fear.

Inez touched Dan's arm. Her eyes were fixed on the youth's face.

'He was one of them,' she said.

The youth's mother heard the accusation and alarm flared afresh in her face.

Dan stepped forward and, resisting the appeals of the boy's mother, he drew back the bedclothes. As he expected, a blood-soaked bandage was tight about the boy's chest.

'Did you get the bullet out?' he enquired.

'He's shot clean through,' said the woman. 'He's lost a lot of blood.'

'Is there a doctor here?'

'No.'

'Have you any flour?'

'A little.'

'Use it to pack the wound. It might stanch the blood-flow. Then tightly wrap him in something clean.'

There was a hint of reluctance in the way the woman set about obeying Dan's instructions, wary lest he was seeking a cruel way to end her son's life, but for the following ten minutes she tended him as instructed.

She wasn't the only one who questioned Dan's mercy.

'He attacked my home,' hissed Inez, 'wounded my father and kidnapped my brother and you offer him comfort.'

'He might have the information we need,' said Dan. He noted the hatred in the flash of the girl's eyes, the same look she had had when attempting to stab him. 'If he dies he won't be able to tell us anything.'

Those words had an effect on Inez. Reluctantly, she inclined her head in a gesture that denoted acceptance of his argument, but her hand still rested on the butt of the pistol she'd collected at the farm.

Sleep, exhaustion or the body's defence mechanism against intense pain had taken the boy's senses and he lay quiet and unseeing on the bed. Once more his mother applied a cold cloth to his brow. After a moment she sent the old woman to the well to bring fresh water.

When she'd gone she spoke urgently to Dan Calloway.

'You want to know where to find Dick Lazarus?'

Dan nodded.

'If I help you will you let my boy live? He's a good boy.'

It was clear that she had a litany of graces to offer on her son's behalf but Inez interrupted the flow.

'He is not good. My father was left for dead and my brother abducted. They stole our animals because they think they are strong enough to take whatever they want. They can't. I will kill Dick Lazarus and all those who help him.'

The mother bowed her head; tears, she knew, might have had some affect on the man but they were useless as a weapon against another woman.

Dan Calloway grasped the girl's arm and drew her towards him, then he spoke to the mother.

'If you know where we'll find Lazarus then tell us and we'll leave you to nurse your son.'

Inez prepared to argue but a harsh look from Dan stilled her.

'I don't know where Dick Lazarus hides,' the mother admitted, 'but the man who was here when you killed Suarez, Hank Garuder, has a cabin along the Tonto Rim. He is a bad man. Lures our young girls with false tales of riches to work in American saloons and our young boys to steal cattle and horses. He tempted my Carlos, then brought him back as you see him.' She looked at her son lying comatose on the bed, noted the shallowness of his breathing and turned again to Dan Calloway as though expecting him to tell her that all would be well.

Instead, he took Inez by the arm and drew her outside.

'Let's go,' he said. 'We'll get nothing more here.'

6

They reached the Rio Bravo by nightfall but deferred crossing into Texas until the following morning. At first, Inez Robles had been annoyed by Dan's sudden withdrawal from the Mexican village. In her opinion, in her quest for justice for the attack on her family, the youth's wound didn't lessen his share of guilt, so she had expected Dan Calloway to exact some greater retribution.

'At the least,' she complained, 'you could have waited to question him. He might know exactly where we'll find Luis.'

'I'm sure he does,' replied Dan, 'but he won't tell anyone. He's lost too much blood. He won't recover consciousness. He'll be dead by morning.'

'Are you sure?'

'I'm sure.'

'But you tried to help him. Tried to stanch the blood loss.'

'That was for his mother's benefit,' he told her. 'In circumstances like this you gain more if you keep a cool head. You have to give a little in order to get a little. She'd told me earlier that Hank Garuder was a bad man. I figured that with a bit of encouragement she'd tell me where to find him.'

Inez was prickled by the criticism; she knew that she had a fiery temper over which, at times, she had little control. It had been the subject of family comments and teasing since childhood, but Dan Calloway's remark about keeping a cool head discomfited her in a new kind of way. She was embarrassed by the jibe but unable to accept it in silence.

'We should have forced the information from him,' she said.

'What good would that have done? If he'd died while we were questioning him we wouldn't have got anything from his mother. A show of force doesn't always work. It's the same with all battles, you have to know which tactic will bring the best result.'

They rode on in silence for a few moments, then Dan spoke again.

'Talking of battles,' he said, 'do you know how to use that?' He indicated the pistol she'd taken from the Suarez farm.

'I know how to shoot a gun.'

'I'm sure you do, but you're wearing it as though you are the fastest draw since John Wesley Hardin. Slung low on your thigh like that suggests you are looking for trouble.'

'I'm not afraid,' she told him.

'I didn't say you were, but you should be. Right now you're determined to pursue the Lazarus gang until you've killed every one of them, but a just cause isn't a guarantee of success. If they learn of your intention they'll kill you and what benefit will that be to Luis or your parents? You have to plan fights, Miss Robles, not engage the enemy in a blind rage. Disguise your passion, take them by surprise. Whenever possible, you have to pick the time and place that is to your best advantage.'

Inez took little pleasure from Dan Calloway's instruction but she paid heed to his words.

'And another thing,' he added, 'back there I told you to wait at the well while I investigated the house, but you didn't.'

'I don't take orders from you,' she insisted. 'Where you go, I go.'

'No, that's not the way it works. You insisted on tagging along, which means we have to trust each other and work together. I wasn't belittling your usefulness, or trying to protect you, or trying to keep information to myself. When you ride with someone you both have jobs to do. I wanted you to keep an eye on the horses because our horses are important. We can't afford to have them stray or be stolen. When you are someplace that you might have to leave quickly, then someone stays with the horses. On this occasion it was you.'

'And why are you the person who decides who does what?'

'Because, at present, I'm the one with more experience in these matters.' He tilted his head to look at her and offered a gentle smile. 'Can we agree on that?'

Mollified in part by Dan's explanation and in part by the calm, amenable tone in which he couched his words, she was able to return his smile to signify her agreement.

'Good,' he said, 'because if we're going to be trail partners we must always know what the other person is doing. I've known men who've killed their partner by mistake because they haven't been where they were expected to be. I would hate to take Luis back home with you tied over your saddle.'

'I wouldn't like that very much, either,' she told him, and they rode on in companionable silence.

* * *

Having crossed the river, they headed south-east towards the distant high ground that could be observed through the shimmering morning haze. The Tonto Rim was a twenty-mile ridge of red rock that pointed the way from the Rio Grande to San Antonio. It was barren land that had formed part of the customary trading trail used by Apache, Comanche and other tribes, and, indeed, it had been the route of the Spanish conquistadores when they explored eastward from their first settlements. Now, the regular trail lay further south, across terrain more suitable for coaches and wagons. Few people now rode along the Tonto Rim.

To conserve the energy of their horses in the shadeless country they proceeded at little more than walking pace. Throughout the morning the heat of the sun increased until, at midday, finding a small creek at which to replenish their water bottles, they dismounted and rested the animals for an hour. Inez was finding it hard to hide her frustration at the slow progress but it wasn't until they were throwing their saddles over their mounts again that she gave voice to it.

'I suppose the gang, too, will travel at this pace?'

'No. They have the advantage of knowing where they're going and probably have fresh horses waiting at Garuder's place. At the moment, Miss Robles, they have all the advantages. We just have to follow with determination and hope that when we catch them good fortune breaks in our favour.'

'That's your plan?' she asked, not sure whether she meant it as sarcasm or as humour.

'That's it,' he told her.

'How lucky I am to have partnered up with someone experienced in such matters.'

Dan Calloway smiled as he tightened the cinch. 'Come on,' he said, 'Garuder's place can't be much further ahead.'

They found it less than an hour later. The house, outbuildings and corrals were in a wide, flat-bottomed arroyo that stretched south from the wall of the rim. Water ran down from the high ground in a course that was thirty yards from the buildings. The stream was ankle high, sufficient to maintain life in the cooking-pot of this arid land. A dozen horses mingled in one corral while a single, high-spirited, seventeen-hand chestnut stallion occupied another.

While they were yet 200 yards from the house a dog barked, giving notice of their presence. They drew rein and waited. Within seconds a figure emerged from the house: a big man, bulky and heavy whom Dan instantly identified as the man he had seen with Hernandez Suarez. At this distance he knew that Hank Garuder would fail to recognize him but would, most probably, be wary of all strangers. He tugged his hat lower on his brow to hide his identity as long as possible and encouraged Inez to take the lead.

'The more he notices you the closer we'll get before he recognizes me,' he explained as they urged their horses forward.

'*Buenos dias,*' she called when they were within hailing distance.

Garuder, who had watched the approaching riders guardedly, now silenced the dog although its stance remained aggressive. Observing her riding-style, Garuder required nothing more than the tone of that greeting to know that his visitor was a member of a prominent Mexican family. He noted how, with her back ramrod straight, she held the reins lightly in her left hand while her right rested elegantly on her hip. Her dark eyes gazed at him with frankness while a soft, friendly smile tugged at her lips. Garuder was also aware that she was young, attractive and well-formed, a combination that always held his attention. Yet something about the girl seemed at odds with her character, although he couldn't instantly identify it.

'Our horses are weary,' Inez said. 'Perhaps we could exchange them for two of your own?' She turned in the saddle so that she was better able to look over the stock in the corral.

Garuder ignored her enquiry. 'What brings you out here?' he asked. 'Not many people ride the Tonto Rim now. If you're heading for San Antonio there's an easier trail down south.'

'I'm not sure where we're heading,' she replied. Her voice had hardened. 'Perhaps you can give us some directions?'

The dog growled as its head turned towards the second rider who, since coming to a halt, had been a horse-length behind the girl and thus partly hidden from Garuder's sight. He, Garuder, had taken little interest in the man, assuming him to be a servant or a *vaquero* from her family estate, but now, with the man in the act of dismounting without invitation, his sense of danger was aroused.

'Horses,' said Inez Robles, trying to draw the man's attention back in her direction. Instantly aware that her words were a ploy to distract him,

Garuder stepped to one side without answering so that he could better see the man behind. At the same time, however, his brain, working now with its usual impetus for self-interest and survival, picked out that aspect of the girl which was at variance with the character he had at first assumed. A well-bred *señorita* would not wear a gun-belt in such fashion. Instinct told him that this was no chance visit.

'Who are you?' he asked, then, as Dan Calloway came fully into view and lifted his head to show his face, he answered his own question. 'You!'

Garuder's hand dipped for the gun in his holster but he was too slow. Once more he found himself under threat from Dan's revolver and ended the draw before he'd got his gun clear. The dog at his side was growling, saliva dribbling from its jaws.

'If that dog makes a move I'll kill it,' Dan warned Garuder. 'Now throw your weapon over yonder.'

Garuder obeyed, discarded the gun

and with a short piece of rope tied the dog to a post.

'What do you want?' he asked.

'I want to know where we'll find Dick Lazarus.'

'I don't know.'

'Of course you know.'

'I haven't seen him since crossing the Rio Grande. He didn't come here.'

'You are a liar,' said Inez Robles. She didn't wait for him to deny it but pointed to the corrals and spoke again. 'That stallion is ours; it was stolen during the raid on my home.'

Dan Calloway didn't want Inez to talk so freely, didn't want her to confirm that she was a member of the Robles family even if Garuder had already guessed her identity.

'In fact,' he said, 'that stallion is mine, as were two of the other horses stolen on that raid and I want to know where they are.'

'I don't know what you're talking about,' grumbled Garuder.

'Of course you do, and when we get

you to San Antonio we'll prove that you are one of the Lazarus gang. The law has been trying to catch up with that gang for some time and I've no doubt that they will be keen to make an example of you in an effort to deter future raids. They'll hang you, Garuder.'

The big man pretended indifference but he couldn't disguise the flare of fear that blazed briefly in his eyes.

'Where is my brother?' demanded Inez.

Garuder glared in her direction and spat on the ground.

'Help yourself, Garuder,' Dan advised. 'Tell us what we want to know and when we hand you over to the sheriff our testimony will surely save your neck. But if I don't get my horses and she doesn't get her brother back safe and sound we'll be happy to return to San Antonio to watch you swing on the gallows.'

Garuder remained silent although it was clear he was weighing his options.

Dan spoke to Inez Robles. 'While I'm

securing our prisoner, put a bridle on the stallion. We'll take him with us.'

'Do you mean to make him talk?' she asked, indicating Garuder.

'I don't think he wants to. He'd rather hang.'

'Then you put a bridle on the stallion and leave him to me.' She slipped down from the saddle and the knife that had appeared in her hand in the bedroom at Pedro's cantina was there again. 'I will make him talk.' She advanced with purposeful stride and with such a look of cold intent that it was clear that no quarter would be given.

Garuder stepped back and cast a look at Dan Calloway that begged for his intervention.

'Let me secure him for you,' Dan told Inez. To Garuder he said, 'I hope she doesn't begin until I'm down there with the stallion. She does dreadful things with that knife.'

'You can't let her kill me,' pleaded Garuder.

'Oh, you'll be pleased when she does.

Believe me, at her hands I've seen men in indescribable torment.' He produced a strip of rawhide with which to secure Garuder's hands.

'No,' said Garuder. He tried to escape but once again Dan was too quick for him, tripped him so that he sprawled full length on his back.

In an instant Dan was on top of him, pinning him to the ground. Over Dan's shoulder Garuder could see the girl with the long slim blade held lightly but threateningly in her hand. The dog, which had grown ever more anxious as the situation developed, was reaching a frenzy in reaction to Dan's attack on his master. With growls and yelps it strained in vain at the restraining rope.

'If you've got anything to tell us then now is the time to do it.' Dan offered his advice in a low voice, as though keeping the content of his speech a secret between himself and his prisoner, but he invested it with a note of urgency and a look over his shoulder to emphasize the threat of the hovering girl. As

Inez bent closer, Garuder submitted.

'Lazarus is holed up in Attica,' he declared.

'Where's that?'

'Back near the border, north of your crossing point.'

'With his gang?' asked Dan.

'Some of them. The others will be scattering the horses around the various buyers.'

'And my brother?'

Garuder swallowed hard before answering; the girl's eyes were no less keen than the edge of her knife.

'They have him at Attica. They'll keep him there until the ransom has been paid.'

'A demand has been sent?'

'The Suarez brothers took it. They were returning home when they caught you. Perhaps they wouldn't have troubled you if they hadn't heard a rumour that you were hunting for Lazarus. Who knows? Hernandez thought that another ransom was too good a chance to miss.'

Dan Calloway stood and told Inez to

put away the knife. With a great show of reluctance she obeyed. They left Hank Garuder lying on the ground while they discussed their next move, moving several yards away because of the barking of the dog.

'Do you believe him?' asked Inez.

'You frightened him enough to make him betray his mother,' said Dan, then confided, 'You frightened me, too.'

'He deserves to die,' she said.

'Perhaps, but we have to release him.'

'Why?'

'Because we don't know where the nearest law office is and we don't want to ride into Attica with Garuder our prisoner. That would advertise our presence to the Lazarus gang.'

'If we let him go he might try to warn Lazarus.'

'We'll tie him up. By the time he works himself free we'll be too far ahead to make pursuit worth while. If he's wise, he'll take the opportunity to quit the territory.'

'We could kill him,' she declared and

there was such a glint in her eye that for a moment Dan suspected that she wasn't joking.

'Let's just revert to the original chores,' he told her. 'You put a bridle on the stallion and I'll secure Garuder.'

They set about their tasks, Inez going down to the corral while Dan hunted out some rope with which to constrain their captive. Returning to the spot where Garuder still sat on the ground, Dan noted the fact that the dog had ceased its struggles and was lying with its head on its front paws. It watched him closely, then looked at Garuder, awaiting the next command.

While Dan and Inez had been in conversation something occurred that gave Garuder hope of gaining the upper hand. So fiercely had the dog struggled against its leash that it had almost pulled the post out of the ground. Consequently, with a quietly issued command, he had ordered the dog to rest and adopt the position in which Dan now found it. After another three steps he had his back to the dog and it was at that point that Garuder gave a low whistle. The dog bounded forward a with such ferocity that the stick was plucked from the ground and flew in the animal's wake as it leapt at Dan's back. The impact knocked Dan forward, unbalanced him and pitched him on to the ground.

The weight of the dog and the surprise of the attack put Dan at an immediate disadvantage. He could feel the claws scratching through the material of his shirt and piercing his skin. The animal's mouth was on the back of his neck and it was trying desperately to sink its teeth into him. He yelled and used his elbow against the dog's head, shifting it momentarily but knowing that it would attack again. He twisted his upper body, tried to turn so that he could better protect himself but the weight of the animal made it difficult. He used both elbows, first the left and then the right to unsettle it and with a determined effort turned his body sufficiently to enable him to throw a solid punch at the dog's head.

He still held on to the rope with which he had intended to bind Garuder and, holding the coil in both hands, stretched it across the animal's face, forcing it into its mouth so that it had to retreat to relieve the pressure. Its feet, however, were on Dan's chest now and they were clawing through his clothing, tearing great rips in both shirt and skin.

Baffled by the rope, the dog attempted to shake it free but Dan managed to keep it tight across its mouth, digging it into the fleshy junction of the lips, making the animal whine with discomfort. It shook its head vigorously from side to side but was unable to escape the rope except by total retreat.

A gunshot sounded, then a second, but Dan couldn't allow them to break his concentration. He was already in a fight that he couldn't afford to lose and to the best of his knowledge the bullets hadn't come in his direction. The name

Inez flashed in his mind but at that moment the dog renewed its efforts and rammed its head into his fac, showering him with its saliva. Twisting his hands, Dan wrapped the rope around the dog's mouth in such a way that he was able to fasten it tightly. The dog was now frightened and struggling to break free, so Dan, gambling that the dog had had enough, did the trick for it.

With a mighty heave he threw the animal away from him, pulling the rope as he did so. This twisted the dog's head, opened its mouth and release the rope from between its teeth. It crashed to the ground several yards away, yelped with pain, then struggled awkwardly to its feet. It shook its head and body as though shaking off river water, then fixed its eyes on Dan who had now got to his knees no less awkwardly than the dog had got to its feet.

The dog launched itself across the space between them, giving Dan no time to defend himself. A gunshot sounded. The dog dropped like a toppled tree and lay dead mere inches from Dan. Ten yards away Inez held a smoking revolver.

'I told you I can use a gun,' she told him.

Dan looked around. 'Those other shots?' he asked, wondering what had befallen Hank Garuder.

'Garuder shot at me when he saw me coming to help and I fired back. We both missed but he's gone.' She pointed to a horse and rider heading west along the Tonto Rim.

7

Although Hank Garuder had gone ahead to warn Dick Lazarus that pursuers were close at hand, Dan Calloway gave no thought to quitting his mission. It meant, however, that the risk to himself and Inez Robles had greatly increased. Surprise had always been the main weapon in the quest to rescue Luis Robles, but that had now gone. Lazarus and his men would be watchful, and ruthless if they discovered the pair. For himself, Dan was determined to press ahead with his quest. He had promised Señor and Señora Robles that he would bring their son home and he had no intention of going back on his word. He had also promised to send their daughter home, but in that he had so far failed. Now, he was compelled to steer her to safety. He believed he had the right argument with which to win her over.

'If things go wrong,' he told Inez, 'what we know will die with us. So we need to split up. I'll chase Garuder while you ride on to San Antonio to raise the Texas Rangers. Then head for home. If I fail or if they elude the Rangers by crossing into Mexico, then perhaps you'll get another chance to capture them when they arrange to exchange Luis for the ransom.'

'No,' she said, resisting that proposal with marked determination. 'You can't shake me off like that. When you confront the Lazarus gang I will be at your side.'

Dan had expected her to reject the proposal, so he was able to explain his motive without any display of frustration.

'This isn't just about Luis; the Lazarus gang have to be stopped. We may not be able to do that alone, especially if they are waiting for us.'

'You're wrong,' she answered. 'As far as I'm concerned this is just about the attack on my family. I know that other people have suffered at their hands and that more will do so if their raids are allowed to continue, but I'm determined that they will be stopped and that I will be there when they are.'

'I believe you, but informing the Texas Rangers will guarantee the end of the gang, no matter what happens to us.'

'Then you go to San Antonio,' she told him, 'but I am heading for Attica.'

'Inez . . . ' he began in protest. Assuming an autocratic posture, she silenced him.

'It is Miss Robles.' She tilted her head so that her dark eyes looked directly into his own. Then they softened as she became aware that he didn't deserve such a high-handed attitude. She rued her obstinacy even though she wouldn't relent. 'You don't have to protect me,' she said and pointed at the dead dog. 'Have I not proved that I am capable with a gun?'

Dan nodded and although there were words of argument waiting to spill from his mouth, he held on to them and with a gesture invited the girl to mount up.

She touched his arm. 'My friends call me Inez,' she said, 'and if we are trail partners then I suppose that makes us friends.'

'If you are as awkward with other people as you are with me I don't imagine you have many.'

They smiled at each other. 'I know you don't want me to get hurt,' she said, her voice gentle to cement the reconciliation, 'but I wouldn't be my father's daughter if I didn't uphold the honour of the family.'

'I don't think your death will add to your father's pride.'

★　★　★

They left Garuder's place on the horses on which they had ridden in. Inez wouldn't leave her palomino and vouched for its stamina. Dan decided that the horses in the corral were an unknown quantity, with every chance that they had recently been more hard-ridden than his own. They also left the stallion in the corral. Now that Hank Garuder was somewhere on the trail ahead, they needed to travel cautiously: trailing the chestnut could be a needless encumbrance.

It didn't escape Dan's thoughts that Garuder, knowing the territory, could be waiting to ambush them. As they rode his eyes scanned every ledge, crevice, high boulder and plateau, watching for telltale movement, rock slips or sunlight reflections that would give warning of a sniper. However, nothing presented itself and they made steady progress on their way to Attica. As they hadn't passed through any settlement on their journey from Mexico, when they reached the point where they had joined the Tonto Rim, they stayed on the high ground instead of retracing their tracks down towards the border. They rode on for another hour before, at the top of a short, steep rise, they halted.

Before them was a wide plateau. Set

back at the furthest point from the edge of the mountain were the first signs of man's existence that they had seen since leaving Garuder's place. A low building of stout timbers was tucked under a colossal overhang so that it was in the shade for most of the daylight hours. Thirty yards to the left an opening in the mountain wall was supported by props of stout timbers similar to those from which the house had been constructed. Painted on the crossbeam in large white letters was one word: ATTICA. Dan and Inez had expected to find a small settlement; instead they'd found a defunct mine.

For a moment they remained motionless, then caution prompted Dan to turn his horse and dismount out of sight of the cabin. When he suggested that Garuder might be inside, looking at them along the barrel of a rifle, Inez copied his example. The place appeared to be deserted, however, and unless his horse was hidden inside the mine Garuder was not here. The evidence that they had been tricked by Garuder wasn't easy to digest. Now they had no idea where to find Dick Lazarus or where Luis was being held captive.

'What do we do now?' asked the girl.

'Look for tracks or some sign that someone passed this way recently,' said Dan. 'If we don't find anything then we need to backtrack to find where he left the rim.'

'Look!' Inez pointed towards the house. The door had opened and a woman in a drab grey dress had taken half a dozen steps in their direction. When she was convinced she had been seen, she beckoned.

'Stay here,' said Dan. Then, knowing the girl's predilection for ignoring his advice, he explained: 'I need you to cover me. This could be a trap. Watch the window and door for anyone with a weapon and yell a warning at the first sign of trouble.'

Without argument she obeyed, drew her gun and from the cover of the hillside observed the building while

Dan walked forward.

The woman was of average height and, despite the plainness of her apparel, had a stately bearing that was diminished by a slight stoop, as though she had carried a vast burden beyond her endurance. Her face was handsome but her brow was furrowed with deep lines that had not been brought about by age; Dan suspected she had barely seen forty years. Her hair, however, was prematurely streaked with grey and her hands were rough and grubby in the manner of one who has laboured to survive. Her lips were thin and dry and her narrowed eyes were green.

'Who are you?' she asked.

'My name is Dan Calloway. Are you alone?'

'Yes.'

Dan looked towards the house and was convinced that it was now empty because neither movement nor sound reached him from within.

'Is this your home?'

'Such as it is now, yes.' She paused,

then corrected herself. 'No, it's my prison.'

'Are you held here by force?'

'By circumstance,' she declared. 'Why don't you tell your lady friend to join us? I haven't spoken to another woman for a long time.'

Once more Dan scanned the house; then, satisfied, signalled for Inez to come forward. The woman was called Mary Cookson and they listened attentively to the story she was desperate to share.

'My husband, John, searched for precious metal all of his life,' she told them. 'Here and there he found pockets of gold or silver, which never amounted to the bonanza he was seeking but were enough to feed us and encourage him to seek further afield. When he found this vein of silver he thought his luck had changed; when the cabin was built I came out here with our son, Tommy, who, at seventeen, was old enough to work alongside his father. Although this strike didn't fulfil John's expectations it still yielded our biggest payload. They worked the mine for a full two years.

'About a year ago John believed the vein was almost played out, that the next load of ore we took down to Laredo would be the last. We planned to go to San Francisco to live the genteel life he'd always promised me. Then Hank Garuder arrived, expressing surprise that we had been here for two years without his knowledge, stressing what a wonderful place this was for avoiding the annoyance of nosy neighbours.

'It was clear that he was bad news, leering at me with such naked intent as to frighten me more than I had ever been in my life. John told him to leave, which he did, but two days later he returned with two companions. From the outset they made it clear that they had come to stay, that they meant to commandeer our home, use it as a hideaway and us as their servants. John protested, ordered them to ride on, so they shot him dead. There was no warning, no mercy; although he was unarmed they killed him in front of his wife and son.'

'Did Garuder kill him?' asked Dan.

'No. It was Dick Lazarus,' replied the woman. 'He is a beast,' she added. 'They are all beasts but he is the worst.'

'You are sure it was Dick Lazarus?'

'Yes. I had seen his likeness in newspapers and on posters. A big man with a scar.' She ran a finger down the side of her face to indicate its location. It was a description that matched that given by Inez of the man who had clubbed and captured Luis.

Dan looked around at the desolate scene. If Dick Lazarus and his gang had used this site as their hideaway there was no evidence of that fact now. The house stood stark and silent against the hillside, without any sign of industry or livestock to relieve its desolation.

'How long did they remain here?' asked Dan.

'They are still here,' the woman replied, but when Dan's hand dropped

to his holstered gun as though antici-
pating the emergence of armed men
from the house she reached out to
prevent him drawing it. 'I mean that
they come whenever it pleases Lazarus
to do so. He descends upon my home
without warning, uses it as though it
was a boom-town beer hall and subjects
me to his vile debauchery.'

Inez stiffened and scowled, shocked
by the woman's sad testimony.

'Why don't you leave?' Dan asked.

'On what?' Angered by the woman's
plight, Inez's voice was thick with
sarcasm. It was clear that there were no
animals around to carry Mary Cookson
from her isolation.

'It's not the loss of the horses that
keeps me here,' said Mary. 'I would
have walked off the mountain long ago
if they had been the only things taken
from me, but they also have my son.
Not content with killing my husband
and abusing me, Dick Lazarus has
forced my son to ride with him, has
made him part of his gang. If I don't

obey Lazarus he will kill Tommy and Tommy knows that my life is forfeit if he doesn't do as he is bid. Lazarus has made us surety for each other. I have told Tommy to forget me, to escape whenever the opportunity arises, but he is a good son and won't put me in danger. He doesn't know,' she added, 'the trials to which I am already put.' She sighed and tears welled in her eyes.

Inez Robles put an arm around the woman's shoulders with the intention of comforting her and leading her back to the house.

'Hank Garuder!' It was Dan Calloway who spoke, anxious not to lose sight of their reason for being at that place.

'Yes,' said Mary Cookson, 'he comes here when Lazarus is away. I tried to resist him but he beat me. One day he will be punished but I don't know that I will be alive to see it.'

Although Dan was concerned for the woman's plight he'd had a more specific reason for speaking of the man who'd escaped their clutches.

'Has he been here today?'

'No. He hasn't been here for several days.'

This was not the answer that Dan Calloway had hoped for and the expression on Inez Robles's face showed disappointment too. Garuder had given them the slip somewhere along the rim. Now they had to retrace their steps and hope to find a trail they could follow. Without it, their hopes of finding Dick Lazarus were greatly reduced.

'Does Lazarus have any other hideaways?' Inez asked the woman.

'Of course,' she replied. 'Other remote homes have been pressed into unwilling service on both sides of the border.'

Dan thought of the Mexican woman who had steered them towards Hank Garuder and knew Mary Cookson's words to be true.

'Do you know where Lazarus will be now?'

She shook her head. 'But when he's here,' she told Dan, 'his men spend their money in Basin Bend. It's a one-street town on the way to Laredo.'

'Do you think he'll be there?'

'I don't know, but you might find Garuder there, or some of Lazarus's men.'

The woman's words carried little more conviction than a hope that she was putting them on the right track, but it was the only clue they had; so, after watering their horses, they rode down from the high ground back towards the trail, where they would look for Garuder's tracks.

'Look out for my boy,' Mary Cookson said as they prepared to ride away. 'He's not a bad boy even though he's riding with those men. Send him home if you find him.'

They had ridden only a hundred yards when Dan turned to Inez and, seeing a troubled expression on her face, asked her to explain its meaning.

'I told you what happened when our home was attacked,' she answered, 'and how Luis fired his rifle until it was empty. He killed three of the bandits. One of them was young boy, not twenty years old. I think her son is already dead.'

8

Such was the clarity of the tracks at the point where Garuder had ridden over the ridge that Dan Calloway was amazed that he'd missed them when passing that point earlier. Even though at that time he had been sure that Attica had been the destination of his quarry, Dan was annoyed by the lapse of concentration. In his haste Garuder had chosen a point to descend where the crust of the surface was too frail to support the weight of a horse; its hoofs, sinking through to a depth of two inches, had gouged great depressions of dust as it had high-stepped, loped, and in some places slithered down the hillside.

Following that trail off the mountain, they discovered, when they reached firmer terrain, that Garuder's horse was carrying a broken shoe which, Inez suggested, might slow him down or even force him to abandon the beast. Dan agreed but pointed out that in those circumstances there was greater likelihood of an ambush and therefore they needed to increase their vigilance. They rode on for several miles until it occurred to Dan that they were not heading in the direction he had expected. According to Mary Cookson, Basin Bend was en route to Laredo, but they weren't going south.

'We're heading for the river,' Dan announced, 'back to Mexico.'

'Is that where they are holding Luis?'

'If Dick Lazarus is still on the other side of the Rio Grande then I guess your brother is there too.'

Twenty minutes later they were forced to reassess their destination. The tracks deviated from the course to the river and turned north-east, towards the Texas panhandle.

'What does it mean?' asked Inez.

'Either Dick Lazarus has another refuge on this side of the border or

Garuder knows someplace where he can swap horses.' Dan favoured the latter explanation because the signs were that the horse with the broken shoe was not travelling well. Its hoof marks were more pronounced, meaning that its pace had dropped, so either it was tiring or the broken shoe was causing it some discomfort.

There was perhaps an hour of light left and Dan was anxious to get as much out of the day as possible, but he was aware that they'd done a lot of hard riding since leaving Garuder's place that morning. Pleading the excuse that they needed to consider the animals, Dan suggested finding a place to bivouac so that they would be more refreshed to continue the pursuit in the morning.

'I think we should keep going until it is too dark to see the tracks,' said Inez. 'My horse will be made no less capable in the morning by covering another five or six miles tonight.'

Dan didn't argue, just nudged his

mount forward to follow the tracks. Inez followed but she thought she'd caught a twitch of a smile on his face as he turned away. When she caught up to her companion her tone contained a touch of annoyance.

'You wanted me to say that, didn't you?'

'I expected you to say that,' he told her.

'And do you intend to persist in this childish manner of manipulation?'

'It works,' he said with a grin.

'It won't again,' she told him.

'Good,' said Dan, 'because I don't want to be continually wondering if you need to rest.'

'Don't worry about me,' she told him. 'I'll keep going as long as you do.'

'But I don't want you to do that. We're not competing against each other, we're partners. I expect you to tell me when you're hungry or when you want to rest. You've already proved your determination in this matter, I don't need any other demonstration to convince me. If you exhaust yourself now, when it isn't necessary, you might not have the reserves to persevere when it is. Besides,' he added, 'the horses do need consideration. It wouldn't help our cause if we lost one or both mounts out here in the Texas scrubland.'

'What will it take for you to stop acting like my nursemaid?'

'A promise that you'll act sensibly, not drive yourself to your limits without due cause.'

Almost scornfully, she replied, 'I promise,' then added, 'and I can assure you that for the next hour or so I will not fall from my saddle in a state of exhaustion nor will little Sierra collapse under me. So lead on, there's no need to stop while there's light left in the day.'

'Stop!' exclaimed Dan. 'I never had any intention of stopping before nightfall.' He grinned at her before upping his horse's pace to a canter.

'I don't suppose you have many friends, either,' she called across the widening gap.

They rode for less than another hour. A little more than a mile ahead the whinny of a horse carried to them from beyond a ridge they were climbing. They dismounted, tethered their own mounts to low shrubs and went ahead, cautiously, on foot. At the lip of the ridge they lay flat, removed their hats and took in the scene before them.

The land dropped away sharply to a depth of twenty feet or more into one of the sudden chasms that characterize that part of the country. This one was also a water course: a thin stream, no more than two yards wide, lay at the bottom. Garuder's horse, a front leg bent so that only the tip of its foot touched the ground, had his head lowered to drink from the slow flow. Someone was removing the saddle from its back, but it wasn't the man who had ridden it pitilessly to this point.

Hank Garuder was in earnest conversation with three other men. One of them, as Inez Robles was swift to point out, wore a Confederate grey jacket and a small forage cap of the same uniform.

'The Lazarus gang,' she hissed.

'Some of them,' agreed Dan. Then he pointed to a corral that had been erected a hundred yards upstream. Ten horses were enclosed, more than was adequate for the number of men below.

'I recognize some of those animals. They belong to my father.' Inez's words confirmed what Dan Calloway had assumed. 'What are we going to do?' she asked.

'I'm not sure,' confessed Dan. 'Lazarus isn't among those below.'

'Perhaps he's coming here,' suggested Inez. 'Why else would Garuder come here?'

'To change horses.' After a moment he spoke again. 'For the moment I think we should wait to see what Garuder does.'

'If he rides on now,' Inez said, 'he'll have a fresh horse. We'll never catch him.'

'I don't think he has any immediate plans to move out,' said Dan.

Using his saddle for a seat, Garuder was now sitting at the side of the stream. After removing his boots he put his feet in the cold water and was continuing his conversation by throwing words over his shoulder.

'I think he's here for the night,' Dan told Inez, 'which suits us fine. We need to rest; by morning we'll be ready to follow him wherever he leads.'

'What if he just came here to leave a message for Lazarus? Perhaps if he leaves in the morning he'll be returning to his home.'

'That's a chance we have to take, but we'll know soon enough if that's his intention. When he cuts south towards the Tonto Rim we'll come back here and take our next cue from the actions of the others.'

'You'll let Garuder escape?' The Mexican girl couldn't hide her displeasure at such an outcome.

'We won't waste time on him at the

moment,' said Dan. 'The Texas Rangers will pick him up when we get a report to them.'

Inez was quiet, reflective, and Dan wondered if she was irked by his comment about the Texas Rangers, or if she had taken his words as a criticism for not riding to San Antonio to summon them. When she spoke, however; it was clear that her mind had been wrestling with the safety of her brother.

'We don't seem to be getting any closer to finding Luis,' she said. 'We don't know what is happening to him or where he is. I was hoping that Garuder would lead us to him.'

'He still might,' said Dan trying to instil optimism in the girl even though it was something that was becoming increasingly difficult to justify. He knew that time was not on their side and, if Garuder got word to Lazarus that he was being hunted, then Luis's life would instantly be ended and the gang members would flee to their hideaways until the next raid was organized.

'He is still alive,' insisted Inez, as though rejecting Dan's unspoken thoughts. 'I'm sure he is.'

Dan thought about the ransom demand that had been delivered by the Suarez brothers to the hacienda of Señor Robles and wondered how the family had reacted to it. It was possible that an exchange had already been arranged and Luis Robles would soon be free. He kept the thought to himself because he suspected that Inez would interpret any mention of the ransom as a plea for her to go home to her family. Indeed, he still believed that that was the safest place for her but knew it wasn't a viable proposition. He wasn't prepared to let her travel alone; for better or worse he had to keep her at his side until he was in a position to escort her home.

As Inez carefully watched the movement of the people in the camp below, so Dan studied her face and for the first time wondered if his reason for keeping her at his side was selfish. At another time and in another place her beauty, undiminished by the dirt, grime and weariness of travel, would surely have dominated his assessment of her, but now he knew there was so much more to her character. For the pampered daughter of a Mexican landowner, her thoughts and actions betrayed an unexpected streak of independence and although her behaviour was sometimes rash it was not without purpose. She was bright, intelligent and full of determination; a loyal fighter.

'Did you see that?' she suddenly said.

'What?'

'The man who came out of the that tent was carrying a plate and cup.'

The tent was little more than a heavy tarpaulin thrown over a high rope slung between two slender river-bank trees, then pegged to the ground to form a shelter. Dan had assumed their provisions were stored in there because it wasn't big enough to be used for sleeping quarters for four men.

'So?'

'He didn't take them in with him,' she said, 'which probably means there is someone in there.'

The girl's assessment caused Dan to scrutinize the camp more carefully.

'Could be Dick Lazarus,' he suggested but instantly rejected that thought. 'No, Garuder would have reported to him as soon as he reached the camp but he hasn't been anywhere near that tent.'

'Perhaps they have a prisoner in there,' said Inez, her large eyes fixed on Dan, hoping for his agreement, desperate to believe that they had found her brother.

Although he told Inez there was no certainty that the person under the tarpaulin was her brother, it was simply to rein in her enthusiasm so that together they could plan what to do next. In fact, Dan was almost as convinced as the girl that Luis Robles was held prisoner by this group of the Lazarus gang. They had, after all, chased Hank Garuder here in the belief that he would lead them to the prisoner and the only negative point was the absence of Dick Lazarus.

Dusk had fallen suddenly as it always did in that territory. Dan led Inez back down to the place where they'd tethered the horses. They couldn't make a fire to brew coffee so their meal consisted of hardtack and water, but the buoyancy of their spirits made light of such meagre fare.

'When it's dark and they are asleep I'll go down and investigate,' Dan said.

'I'm coming with you,' said the girl.

'No. You have another job to do. If we rescue Luis we'll need another horse. Can you cut one out of the corral and bring it back here without being discovered?'

'Why don't you do it and I'll free my brother?'

'Because we still don't know that Luis is there, and even if he is we don't know what condition he's in. He may need help to get out of their camp. It's the simple fact that I'm stronger than you if he needs to be carried.'

'You always have a reason, don't you?'

'Yes,' he said, 'and I have reason for saying that now we should get some sleep.'

'Sleep? I can't sleep.'

'Perhaps not, but you must still lie down and rest. We can't do anything until their camp is quiet and we'll need to be alert and ready to ride hard if we rescue Luis. We'll want to cover a lot of ground before they discover he's gone.'

The night was warm and sleeping under the stars with a saddle for a pillow wasn't a hardship. Despite her insistence that she wouldn't be able to sleep, Inez Robles did so for more than an hour. When she awoke she glanced at the blanket-covered form of Dan Calloway lying some yards away. He was on one side with his back to her and motionless except for the heaves caused by regular breathing. She didn't think he was asleep but in the darkness all things were vague and confused. For several moments she waited, partly because she was anxious to be under way with their plans, yet enjoying a sense of security, as though the night had combined with some unknown force to form a cocoon of contentment around her. She closed her eyes and wallowed in the unexpected pleasure.

'Time to go.' Dan's voice interrupted her reverie but didn't destroy the mood she was experiencing; in fact, it was as though she had been waiting for him to speak and she almost smiled when he did. Inez wondered if she'd dozed again because when she opened her eyes she found that Dan had already rolled up his blanket and was tying it to the back of his saddle.

All was silent in the chasm below. Glowing embers marked the dying remains of the fire around which Garuder and the other outlaws had sat with their coffee and cards. Now they were spread out but in the darkness it was impossible to pinpoint their locations.

Dan led the way, choosing a route which circled the camp so that they could approach the horses from the opposite end. Inez had assured him that the horses from her home would recognize her, that she had worked most of the horses on their estate and knew which would be the most placid when led from the corral. It crossed Dan's mind that he and Inez would benefit from fresh horses, but smuggling away one beast would be tricky enough and the girl would probably protest at the suggestion of leaving behind her palomino, so he kept the thought bottled within himself. It was now too late for discussions or alterations to the plan.

He left Inez at the corral with the instruction to get back to the horses as swiftly and silently as possible.

'If things go wrong,' he told her, 'if they catch me, ride hard for San Antonio. Don't do anything foolish. You'll be the only one capable of guiding the Rangers to this location.'

Then he was gone, silently moving from cover to cover as he approached the outlaws' camp.

The smell of hot coffee floated to Dan as he reached that part of the tarpaulin sheet that formed the rear of the tent. The pot, he figured, had been left on hot stones by the embers to replenish the tin cup of anyone who needed it during the night. For a moment he wondered if a night-guard had been posted, but so still and silent was the area that he dismissed the idea. He edged forward towards the tarpaulin and at that moment the sound of a startled horse carried to him from the corral.

Drawing back from the makeshift tent, he lay flat on his stomach to see what effect the noise would have on the sleepers.

Someone shouted. 'What's troubling the horses?'

A sleepy reply was dismissive of investigation. 'Some of those Mexican horses are so nervous that they are skittered by flies.'

'There aren't any flies out at night,' the first man argued.

'Then it'll be coyotes drinking at the stream. Forget it.'

By this time, the first man had reached the remains of the campfire. A rifle was grasped in his hands and he was peering in the direction of the corral. In a moment he was joined by Hank Garuder. He too was armed. For a minute they stood side by side, but there was no further sound of disturbance.

'I'll take a look,' said the first man. He stepped in Dan's direction. When he reached the tarpaulin he paused and looked inside; then, with a grunt of satisfaction, he continued past the tent on his way to the corral. His route took him within six feet of Dan, who went undiscovered as he lay full length in a fissure in the dry ground.

Dan remained still until the man returned because Garuder had moved forward to stand beside the tent.

'Mort must have been right about the coyote.'

'I'm worried about that fellow who turned up at my ranch,' admitted Hank Garuder. 'He didn't seem like the sort who would give up easily.'

'Relax,' said the other. 'You're as nervous as the horses.'

'Yeah, well Lazarus needs to know about him. I think you should get word to him.'

'I've got my orders. I have to stay here. If you want to cross the river when the sun comes up you'll find him in Vallarta. But he's with the Garibay woman and you won't be a welcome visitor.'

The two men walked away, back beyond the now dead fire, and disappeared into the darkness whence they'd come. Their brief conversation had provided Dan with all the information he required; once he'd got Luis and Inez across the river and safely on their journey home he would notify the Mexican authorities that Dick Lazarus could be found in some place called Vallarta. For now, though, he would have to give the camp time to settle down again before attempting to rescue Luis. This was unfortunate because in this territory the sun came up as swiftly as it went down. He couldn't afford to delay too long. However, he was now convinced that Luis Robles was being held prisoner inside the makeshift tent. The outlaw's brief examination of the interior could only have been to satisfy himself that the noise from the corral had not been instigated by anything that had happened in the camp, and that his prisoner was still secure.

Eventually Dan made his move, crawling forward until he could touch the tarpaulin, then worked his way along the side until he was able to slip inside through the opening. The interior was a small space, the majority of which was taken up by a low couch on which a man was lying. Stealthily, Dan crossed to it. Reaching down he grasped the man's shoulder to shake him awake.

'Luis,' he uttered low and urgently, but the word was lost in the dreadful howl of pain emitted by the other man.

The man on the bed was not Luis. When he sat bolt upright Dan's mistake was obvious. This man was a fair-haired American who cursed in fluent English. He was wounded, probably another casualty of the raid in Mexico, and Dan's attempt to wake him had induced great agony. Clearly, his yells would be heard by those sleeping only yards away and Dan knew he had to get out quickly.

As he quit the tent he could see two figures hurrying towards him. Intending to retrace his steps and perhaps make his escape on one of the horses in the corral, he turned along the side of the tent, where he hoped that for a precious few seconds, he would be obscured from the sight of the outlaws. But in the darkness, and needing to forgo caution, he tripped over one of the pegs that were fastening the tarpaulin to the ground. He stumbled, then fell. Before he could regain his feet one of his pursuers appeared and without a word swung his rifle with terrific force so that the butt crashed against Dan's head, rendering him unconscious to lie full length on the ground.

9

With his returning senses, the pain in Dan's head increased. He moaned. He would have raised a hand to examine the damage done by the rifle butt but that wasn't possible. He was sitting on the ground, bound to a tree with his hands secured behind his back. The darkness of the night was illumined by a flaming brand, below and behind which five faces glowered at him. One of those faces belonged to Hank Garuder, who was loud in his demands for Dan Calloway's death.

'You said he had a girl with him,' someone answered. With a grimace, Dan raised his head and saw that the speaker was the man in the Confederate jacket. 'We need to know where she is.'

'What does it matter?' argued Garuder. 'A girl on her own isn't capable of hurting us.' His eyes met Dan's and instantly he understood the message that Dan flashed at him: that that same girl had terrified him only hours earlier. Clearly, however, that message was unnecessary. Despite Garuder's brutish words, his voice was edged with desperation and nervousness, as though he was anxious to have all trace of that earlier meeting eradicated. The story he had told these men about the confrontation at his home had not contained any mention of his humiliation at the hands of a woman, and what he yearned for now was the elimination of Dan and Inez at the earliest possible opportunity to prevent any word of it spreading among these associates. The man in the Confederate jacket spoke.

'Let's hear what he's got to say.' He kicked Dan's feet to get his attention. 'Why are you chasing us? Are you the law?'

'You stole my horses.'

'Your horses? We sell horses to Americans, we don't steal them on this side of the river.' His words brought a few laughs from those gathered around.

'Even so,' Dan told him, 'some of the animals you've got in that corral belong to me. I bought them from Señor Robles.'

'According to Garuder, the girl is the daughter of this man Robles, is that right?'

Dan offered no reply.

'The word from San Miguel is that when she finds us she will kill us.' When Dan still remained silent, his questioner spoke again. 'We're very frightened.' He pretended to shiver to emphasize the point. This provoked more laughter, but Garuder didn't join in. 'So where is she?'

'Where do you think she is?'

The man looked around at his companions as though surprised by Dan's response. Without warning, he lashed out with his foot and kicked Dan in the ribs, driving the breath from his body and inflicting intense pain. Then he crouched, grabbed a handful of Dan's hair and pulled back his head so that they were nose to nose.

'You're not in any position to ask questions,' he snarled. 'I ask, you answer. Now, where is the girl?'

'Some place that you can't reach her.'

The man jagged Dan's head back against the tree to which he was tied. Pain and nausea almost swamped Dan's senses but he still heard his inquisitor's voice through the dizzying fug.

'Where is she?'

'Gone,' Dan said.

'Gone where?'

'San Antonio, to summon the Rangers.'

The man's laugh was intended to show his derision of the Rangers. 'What will they do? We'll be gone from here before they can organize a posse.'

'Gone from here perhaps, but you won't be able to use Garuder's place again, nor Attica.'

'Attica! What do you know about Attica?'

'Just what Garuder told us.'

The man released his hold on Dan's

hair and turned his attention to Hank Garuder. 'How many other places did you tell them about?'

'None,' answered Garuder.

Dan, fighting his pain and wooziness knew he had an opportunity to discredit Garuder. He couldn't be certain how the gang would react but at least Inez would be safe. They would be more concerned with their own safety than chasing the Mexican girl who, as far as they knew, was well on the way to San Antonio. He raised his head.

'Basin Bend,' he said.

'I didn't tell him about Basin Bend,' Garuder cried defensively.

'He did. He was keen to talk because the girl terrified him. If I hadn't stopped her she would have cut out his heart.'

'That's not true,' said Garuder, but the fear and anger that showed on his face made it difficult for anyone to attach credence to his denial.

'And across the Rio Grande,' continued Dan, 'there's a place called Vallarta, information which the Rangers are sure to pass on to the *Federales*.'

The inquisitor sprang up and faced Garuder. 'What have you done? What else have told these people?'

'Nothing,' protested Garuder. 'I don't know where he got those names from. Just kill him and be done with it.'

Garuder began to draw his pistol but the other man prevented him, grabbing his wrist until he released his hold on the gun.

'No,' he said. 'Lazarus will want to interrogate this man himself, and perhaps you, too.'

Garuder's protestations of innocence were ignored and the man in the Confederate jacket ordered everyone back to their bedrolls.

'We can still get a couple of hours' sleep before sunup. Brad,' he spoke to the man whom Dan and Inez had seen unsaddling Garuder's horse. 'At daylight you'll take a message to Lazarus while the rest of us move the horses to Cy Major's Flying M ranch up near Rock Springs.'

After Dan's bonds had been checked Mort was ordered to guard him for the remainder of the night. It was not a task to Mort's liking, he looked the most tired of the group, but he rubbed his face with his hands and offered no objection. The dying fire brand was stuck in the ground, and when everyone else was settled he took up a position next to a boulder against which he could rest his back but from which he had a clear view of the prisoner.

Thirty minutes later the torch had burned out and the guard was dozing. Dan was uncomfortable: not only was he in pain from the blows he'd received, but the cord that had been used to bind him was cutting into his wrists as he struggled to manipulate his hands free. From time to time, Mort would rouse himself from the arms of Morpheus, sometimes with a snort, sometimes with a jump and a grumble, but each time, his first conscious thought was to satisfy himself that the prisoner was still securely bound.

Mort had been slumped against the rock now for ten minutes, his arms folded and his chin on his chest. Now and then little snores interrupted his rhythmic breathing, denoting a deeper level of sleep. Dan worked furiously but no matter how much he persevered at the task he had no reward. Whoever had bound him had known their job. He realized that it might be impossible to escape his bondage before daylight but he wasn't prepared to give up. He took a deep breath and prepared to try again. Unexpectedly, from behind, he felt the breath and heard the sound of a whisper in his right ear.

'It's me,' said Inez.

'What are you doing here?' Dan had hoped the girl had witnessed his capture and ridden away to safety.

'I'm disobeying orders again,' she hissed. 'Do you want me to go and guard the horses or cut you free?' She flourished the knife that kept popping out like a rabbit from a magician's empty hat.

With a motion of his head he indicated that she should slice through the cords. At the same time words of chastisement spilled out.

'You should have gone,' he told her. 'It's foolishness to put yourself in such danger.' He felt the cords around his wrists slacken, then his hands were free.

'We're partners, aren't we?' she murmured. 'If I was the captive, you wouldn't have gone without trying to rescue me.'

'That's different,' he said. The ropes that tied him to the tree dropped away.

'No it's not,' she insisted.

That was the last word of the argument because the next voice was Mort's.

'What are you doing over there?' he asked, his question directed at Dan who seemed to be moving more freely. He stood and crossed the space between them, anxious to make sure that the prisoner was still secure. The night was waning but the remaining darkness was still enough to obscure shapes and, because she was lying flat on the ground behind Dan, Mort didn't see Inez at all. She had gathered up the ends of the severed ropes and was holding them so that to any casual glance it appeared as though Dan was still tied to the tree, but Mort had decided that a closer inspection was required.

He bent over and grasped the ropes, gave them a tug, then gasped in surprise. Inez had released her hold and Mort found himself with a handful of rope.

A shout of warning was on his lips, an intended call to rouse the camp that their prisoner was free, but the alarm was never given. Inez had slipped her knife into Dan's hand and, as Mort leant close to examine the rope bonds, Dan had thrust it forward, penetrating the outlaw's clothes, skin and inner organs. He twisted the knife and forced it deeper into Mort's body. Mort gasped, tried to resist, but was dead in seconds.

'Come on,' Dan urged Inez, and began to rise.

'What about Luis?' she asked, but before she received an answer a shot took them by surprise.

The bullet hit the tree to which Dan had recently been tied, ripping off splinters and sending them spinning into the darkness beyond. Inez, obedient to Dan's call, was in the process of rising when a six-inch-long sliver of bark flew past her face, so close that the shock evoked an involuntary squeal.

The prospect of facing Dick Lazarus had made it impossible for Hank Garuder to sleep. Since Jake Stewart, the man in the Confederate jacket, had mooted that possibility, Garuder's mind had been engaged in concocting an explanation for Dan's being in possession of the hideout locations. If Lazarus believed that he was responsible for imparting that knowledge his life would be forfeit. Lazarus didn't allow that sort of weakness in his gang members. So for the past two hours Garuder had been lying uncomfortably in his bedroll; he had only sat up when he heard Mort call to the prisoner.

Garuder watched as Mort crossed to the tree to ensure that Dan Calloway was still securely bound, but when the guard pitched to the ground Hank had known instinctively that he was dead. He could have raised the alarm at that point, shouted a warning to rouse the gang members from their slumber, but it flashed through his mind that if he did so it was likely that Jake would still insist upon taking Dan alive to face interrogation by Dick Lazarus. Such an outcome would still leave Hank in a precarious position. Better by far, he told himself, that Dan Calloway should die, and who would question his motive for shooting him as he attempted to escape?

So Hank Garuder had fired at Dan Calloway, but the dim light and the speed of the escapee's movement meant that he missed the target. It was only when he heard the girl's squeal that he realized that Dan Calloway was not alone.

'The girl's here,' he shouted to the other outlaws who, alerted to the situation by the gunshot, were scrambling out of their bedrolls and reaching for their guns.

Responding to the Mexican girl's squeal, Dan Calloway turned back and saw her fall to the ground. Fearing she had been hit by the bullet he turned back and threw himself to the ground beside her.

'I'm all right,' she told him. 'Just lost my balance.'

More shots followed, some striking the tree, some ricocheting off the hard surface of the ground and yet more flying off into the darkness of the night.

Dan's gun had been taken when he was captured but he remembered the one that Inez carried strapped to her thigh. He took it from her and took aim at the four outlaws coming towards him. He didn't know how many bullets were in the gun; he hoped it was full, but he knew he couldn't afford to waste any. The one advantage he had was that his enemies thought he was unarmed; although the tree that he and Inez lay behind provided little cover, they had none at all. They were advancing openly, confident that he couldn't escape their fusillade.

Dan's first shot hit Brad in the chest, dropping him in his tracks as he clutched his hands to the fatal wound. The second hit Garuder in the forehead, ending for ever his apprehension of a meeting with Dick Lazarus. At the fall of their companions, the other two turned back, seeking cover behind low rocks. For the moment, the roar of the six-guns was silenced.

While the remaining outlaws gave consideration to the situation, Dan took the opportunity to check the loads in his pistol. Three remained. He gave the gun to Inez with the instruction that if they presented a clear target she was to shoot to kill.

'If they shoot at me from cover then

return their fire and make them keep their heads down.'

'What are you going to do?' she asked, anxious lest he intended to put himself in danger in order to protect her.

'Get Mort's gun,' he said, indicating the nearby body of the man who had been posted to guard him. 'It will even up the fight if we all have guns. Are you ready?'

Inez nodded and fixed her sights on the rocks behind which their adversaries were hiding. Dan moved quickly, rolling along the ground until he bumped against Mort's body. From across the clearing a gun was fired. Dan felt the thud of the bullet as it thumped into the body at his side. The answering shot from Inez had the effect that Dan had hoped for: it caused the shooter to retreat, thereby giving Dan the opportunity to pull Mort's gun from its holster. His intention had solely been to get possession of the weapon but now, with the respite from flying lead and the belief that Inez would protect him if his adversaries recommenced the shooting, he began to work at removing the gun-belt from the dead man. The additional ammunition would be a bonus.

He was tugging at the belt when another shot struck the ground close to where he lay. It had been fired from an unexpected direction. One of the outlaws had moved, had taken up a wider position in order to trap them in a crossfire. In confirmation of this assessment, a shot was fired from the original position and Inez replied instantly. If she hadn't reloaded she now had only one bullet left in the gun. Forsaking the belt but slipping four or five cartridges from the loops, Dan flipped a couple as a hint towards Inez.

'Concentrate on the rocks,' he told her, keeping his voice low so that it didn't carry to their enemies. 'I'll take care of the one who is circling.'

With those words uttered he moved behind the tarpaulin, out of sight of

Inez and their attackers. Pistol in hand and slithering snakelike on his stomach, he moved to his right in a line which, he anticipated, would intercept the route of the man on the move. Every now and then, after covering a few feet of ground, he paused, not only to ensure his course was true but also to listen for movement ahead. It was after one such pause that the outlaws launched their attack. If a signal had been given Dan had missed it, but both men began firing at the same moment. The position that Inez held was their target.

Bullets hummed through the air above her head, forcing her to lie flat and seek every inch of cover that the tree provided. Without sight of her attackers she extended her arm and fired twice towards the rocks that she had had under observation, but bullets still came at her from two directions, so she knew that her reply had had no effect. The men continued to advance and were pouring a lot of lead at her.

She had managed to put some fresh

shells into the revolver but she doubted if there was more than two live rounds left. She pulled the trigger until she heard the awful metal click as the hammer hit spent chambers. Someone was only yards from her position now and she had nothing left with which to defend herself.

Although the gunfire that Jake Stewart and his companion had faced had been accurate, it had also been sparse, which led the outlaws to believe that their adversaries were low on ammunition. Splitting up, presenting two fronts that had to be attacked would prove that theory. So he had circled around to his left until he was in a position near the still warm fire, which was twenty yards from the tent and the tree to which their prisoner had been tied.

He fired a shot at one figure who was using Mort's body for protection and saw him scuttle away, presumably to the safety of the tree from where the only shots fired had been in response to those fired from the rocks. He had waited and watched for several minutes, but there had been no movement or attempt to escape. He had them trapped and now was not a time to show mercy. The girl had not gone to fetch the Rangers and any knowledge that the man had would die with him. Their prisoner and the girl had killed three men and Lazarus would not be pleased.

In the gathering light of day, Jake Stewart stormed forward, repeatedly firing the guns in each hand, this being the signal for Ben Fall to begin the crossfire from the rocks. Jake was close enough to hear the telltale clicks of the empty gun and he believed he had his enemies at his mercy. Two steps from the tree he spotted the prone body of the girl. He prepared to pull the trigger and end her life. He was a split second too slow.

Dan Calloway, rising to his feet, barely took aim but his bullet smashed into Jake Stewart's skull, hurling him forward and down so that his shocked face with its bulging eyes landed inches from Inez. Dan turned his attention to the last outlaw who, having seen the fate that had befallen his companions, now stood and cast his gun a distance away. Dan tied his hands and pushed him into the tent alongside his wounded comrade.

'My advice to you,' Dan told Ben Fall, 'is to ride well clear of Texas. The Rangers will soon be scouring this territory and if they find you they'll hang you. If you or your pal try to get word to Dick Lazarus, or if I see you here or in Mexico again, I'll kill you. You can have one horse each. The others you'll leave in that corral for their rightful owner.' He untied Ben Hall, then knocked him unconscious with the pistol he was holding.

Together, Dan and Inez collected all the guns and put them in a sack which they dropped some miles away as they rode to the Rio Grande and recrossed into Mexico.

10

As they rode back across the Rio Grand, Dan was aware of a distinct air of melancholy about the girl. Some of her natural colour had faded and her gaze had dropped to the pommel of her saddle rather than being raised to the horizon as it had been at all other times. Despite her brave talk and actions, the gunfight, he supposed, had had some effect on her but he didn't consider that to be the entire cause of her low spirits.

It seemed as though the new belief that her brother was being held in Mexico had drained her of energy. Vallarta, she had told him, was a town less than thirty miles west of her home, and the realization that Luis had been almost on her doorstep had added an unwelcome emphasis to the sense of time wasted in journeying east across the border.

'We did the only thing we could do,' Dan had told her. 'We followed the clues.' Although she'd acknowledged the truth of his words they hadn't lessened her frustration. It would take another full day of travel to reach their new destination and there was no guarantee that that would be the end of their journey. For several miles they had ridden in silence.

It was late the following morning when they reached the outskirts of Vallarta. It was a larger, more prosperous town than San Miguel, and accordingly boasted a doctor, a lawyer and a minister who conducted services at the little church around which the town had been built. In addition, it was the home of leather workers, cloth dyers, potters and other artisans, as well as those peons who worked the surrounding land, and there were restaurants and cantinas to cater for the needs of those who attended the weekly market. For that part of northern Mexico, it was a thriving community, a condition due, Inez informed Dan, to its former status as a military outpost. Although the army had been withdrawn after the defeat of the French and the execution of the Emperor Maximilian in 1867, the town had continued to be the centre of affairs in that area.

Those substantial buildings that had been the offices and billets from which the affairs of the military had been administered had long since been adapted for civilian use. In these premises the lawyer and the doctor had set up their offices and other rooms had been designated for communal use. The greater part of the site, however, had been converted into a hotel that offered accommodation more grand than could otherwise have been expected. Dan having persuaded Inez that they needed a base from which to operate, it was to this building that they directed their mounts.

'This is a bigger town,' Dan explained. 'If we advertise our mission someone might inform Lazarus before we find him. The element of surprise will be lost. His men might come looking for us. We need to be discreet, keep our eyes open for Americans and hope that one of them leads us in the right direction.'

He knew that this cautious approach was at odds with the girl's anxiety to find her brother swiftly. The frustration caused by delay was close to becoming desperation and that was when mistakes occurred. They were both in need of rest and nourishment although he suspected that such a suggestion would be interpreted as a sop to the weaker sex. However, with little more than a momentary unsure glance, Inez accepted his argument and they went into the hotel.

The clerk, a small, neat man with bright eyes and expressive hand gestures, welcomed them and assigned them to opposite second-floor rooms. He promised to send up hot water to Inez's room and gave Dan directions to a barber-shop.

There was a lot of activity on the street, and it seemed to Dan that most of it involved children. Some were being called and chivvied home, others were on board wagons or rode behind a parent astride horses and mules heading out of town. The children looked happy; the adults less so. It had always been Dan's impression that, generally, the Mexican people tended to be sombre and suspicious, but their recent history had been a series of wars and revolutions, enough to leave a legacy of unease and mistrust for decades to come.

This day, in this town that Inez had described to him as a place of wealth, culture and fun, it felt like a place under threat from an implacable enemy. It wasn't just the parents of the children who wore troubled expressions, they were present wherever Dan looked, on the faces of men and women, shopkeepers, market traders and even those who lounged in the shade.

The barber was little different; indeed, when Dan entered his low, dark building the man's urge to please was conveyed with cowering subservience. He spoke little, babbling in Spanish as though he knew no English, but when Dan queried the number of Americans in Vallarta it was clear that the man understood. His shrug didn't imply that he had no number to impart, more that the question was unexpected and its relevance a riddle. He was even more surprised when, upon his completing his task with the razor, Dan flicked a silver coin to him.

'I need some clean clothes,' Dan said. 'Where is the nearest store?'

The proprietor of the place to which he was directed could have been the barber's brother. Not only was he of similar stature but his demeanour was strikingly similar. At first, the store-keeper was sure that he had nothing that would fit the big American, but Dan's insistence produced a pair of jeans and a red wool shirt that was tight across the shoulders but preferable to the grubby one that hadn't been off his back for five days.

'You are going to the fiesta?' asked the Mexican storekeeper.

Dan confessed that he knew nothing about a fiesta, which seemed to surprise the man. When a further tentative enquiry garnered the knowledge that Dan was new in town and staying at the hotel it brought about a complete change in the storekeeper's manner.

His face registered relief, as though Dan's words had provided testimony to an unexpected innocence. The alteration in the man's manner didn't escape Dan and he wasn't slow in attaching a meaning to it. Both the storekeeper and the barber had expected different behaviour, had been wary of his custom as though it could only bring trouble. They thought he was someone else. That someone, Dan supposed, would be a member of the Dick Lazarus gang.

'Where is the fiesta being held?' he asked.

'Where it is held every year. At the hacienda of General Garibay.'

'Garibay,' repeated Dan. He had heard

that name before, and as he retraced his steps to the hotel he recognized its significance.

★ ★ ★

There had been no time for rest but, by not talking about the fiesta until they were drinking coffee, Dan ensured they had a proper meal before leaving Vallarta.

'Who is General Garibay?' he asked Inez Robles.

'A hero of the war against the French. One of Benito Juarez's most able soldiers. He was responsible for a great victory in Chihuahua.'

'I believe he has a hacienda not far from here.'

'That's true. How do you know?'

'Because there is a fiesta being held there today.'

'Yes,' said Inez after a moment of thought. 'Every year to commemorate his victory he welcomes his neighbours to his home. When I was younger my parents took Luis and me. We haven't been for a few years.'

'I think we should go today.'

'Go to a *fiesta*?' snapped Inez. 'What about Luis. Have we not come to Vallarta to find my brother?'

'Of course we have, and I believe we'll find him at the hacienda of General Garibay.'

'What!'

'I think we'll also find Dick Lazarus there. During the conversation I over-heard when they spoke of Vallarta someone said that Dick Lazarus was with the Garibay woman. That would suggest someone at the general's hacienda.'

'There is only his wife.' A furrow formed across Inez Roble's forehead. 'What does it mean?' she asked, but her troubled face suggested that she was already drawing conclusions.

'Do you know Señora Garibay?'

'We've met. She is much younger than her husband. She has two young children.'

'I think we should get out there as quickly as possible,' said Dan.

Inez was already standing, as though ready to jump into the saddle and kick up dust.

'First,' said Dan in a voice full of quiet authority that induced her to regain her seat, 'we must prepare ourselves as best we are able.'

'You have a plan?'

Dan shook his head. 'It's impossible to plan because we don't know what we can achieve. I think that Luis is being held prisoner there but I can't be sure. I think Dick Lazarus is there, but again, I can't be sure, and if he is I don't know how many men he has with him. I'm guessing there can't be more than six because we've dealt with some and we know that others are somewhere in Texas selling off the stolen horses.'

'Then what can we do?'

'Make some decisions.'

'Such as?'

'Whether or not we arrive together. If Lazarus is aware that you are on his trail in company with an American we'll stand out like buffaloes in a herd of sheep.

'Do you think he knows?'

'It's no more than possible,' confessed Dan, 'but the Suarez brothers and Garuder, too, might have passed on information about you.'

'What do you suggest?'

'Make yourself look as masculine as possible. Wear a poncho and a high sombrero with your hair piled up inside.'

'OK,' she said. 'That way I can wear the gun-belt without arousing interest.'

★ ★ ★

Fifteen minutes later they quit the town on their weary horses. Inez, mounted and camouflaged, attracted no second glances from anyone. Somehow she had acquired a multicoloured poncho of which the length and weight successfully obliterated every trace of her body shape; riding with her shoulders hunched she was the very image of a humble worker. The big straw hat she now wore cast enough shade over her face to hide her features from anything but the most intense scrutiny.

Dan Calloway rejoiced in the fact that the girl had shaken off her recent torpor and had with some alacrity adopted his suggestion, but his pleasure was tempered by her eagerness to reach General Garibay's and the possibility that it was a precursor of rash action. Despite her current behaviour it was clear that she was still governed by the frustration of wasted time and false hopes. He blamed himself for raising her hopes again and worried about the adverse effect if they failed once more to find her brother. For now, though, she was riding at his side in companion-able silence, projecting an aura of expectation, as though the conclusion of an adventure was close at hand.

It was well into the afternoon, much later than the start time of many of the planned events that comprised the fiesta, when they arrived at the estate of General Garibay. Black cannons flanked the high, white-painted, adobe brick gateway. The road beyond disappeared behind a low hill, and the house, Inez explained, lay half a mile ahead on a long plain above the running water of the Rio Conchos. As they rounded the hill they were greeted by a scene which caused both of them to rein their horses to a halt and elicited a gasp of shock from Inez.

From a tree the body of a man was hanging. Not a young man, but one who, in life, had been burly and strong. A trim moustache still showed on a face that was darkening from strangulation.

'It's General Garibay,' said Inez. At that moment both Dan and Inez knew they'd found the lair of Dick Lazarus.

11

'If you two are here for the fiesta then keep moving.' The voice belonged to one of two men who had ridden out from behind a bush, where they had been stationed. They were Americans, rough and unkempt, with the cold, merciless looks of men who rode with death. Each carried an unsheathed rifle and kept a finger inside the trigger guard. If compelled, it was clear that they would use their guns without hesitation.

Beside him, Dan sensed a reaction from Inez, a start of repulsion, anger or fear, and he guessed that she had recognized at least one of the riders from the raid on her home. Dan inclined his head towards the hanging body.

'What happened?'

The taller of the two, a bulky man in

a dirty grey shirt and black trousers, permitted himself a sneer.

'He stole our horses,' he said. 'We hang horse-thieves.'

'That's General Garibay.'

'Sure is. Mexican generals are as dishonest as Mexican peasants.'

The other man, slimmer with deep-set eyes that regarded Dan and Inez from under heavy lids, added an explanation:

'That's because most of them were peasants before the revolution.'

'I'd heard that the general was a man of renown.'

'Yeah! Renowned for rustling horses!' The man laughed and his companion shared in the humour. 'Now, ride on. The new owner enjoys a fiesta, too.'

'Who is the new owner?' asked Dan.

'Don't ask questions, mister. You just spread the word when you leave here that we'll punish in our own way any Mexican that tries to steal American stock.'

Dan felt sure that the disguised girl at

his side was preparing to reject the men's false testimony, but for the moment he didn't want her to reveal herself to them. He nudged his horse forward so that he was between her and the others, then signalled for her to follow him.

'They are liars,' she hissed when they ridden on.

'Of course they are. They are posted there to make sure that everyone hears the same lie — which is meant to justify the killing.'

She withdrew her hand from beneath her poncho. It was holding the pistol.

'We should have killed them,' she said. 'They were part of the gang that raided my home.'

'I figured that you'd recognized them,' said Dan, 'but this isn't the moment to fight. If the sound of gunfire carried down to the hacienda it would forewarn Lazarus of trouble. We don't want that: we want every opportunity to find Luis before we are discovered.'

'I know,' she said, 'but they have

murdered a good man.'

'We'll inform the Federales at the earliest opportunity.'

Inez expressed annoyance. 'Pah! The government no longer upholds those principles for which the general fought. The Federales themselves might have had a hand in this outrage. It would suit the government to have the general's outspoken voice silenced.'

'Mexican politics aren't my concern,' Dan told Inez, 'but it would be interesting to know what reason Dick Lazarus had for killing General Garibay.'

'You know the only reason he needs is that someone has something he wants, and the general would defend his home and his family with his life.'

From ahead came the sound of voices, and although it was generated by a multitude it was a muted sound, lacking in excitement or joy. As the two riders breasted a rise they were able to look down on the compound that was the home of the Garibay family. Buildings formed three sides of a rectangle which was completed at the front by a stout adobe wall. The ornate gates in the centre of this wall were open and led into a courtyard which was adorned with colourful bunting. At the heart of the courtyard could be seen a spectacular fountain, in front of which a dais had been erected upon which was seated a solitary figure.

Surrounding the compound were variously sized corrals. People were sitting or clinging to the bars of the nearest corral, watching as a bull was taunted by a matador in dour black clothing. The people weren't silent but there was no enthusiasm for the event, no shouts of *Ole!* when the bull was duped by the cape and no cheering when, bemused, it stopped charging altogether.

Apart from those areas that had been set aside for the entertainment of children, there was little evidence that the occasion was a source of enjoyment to those in attendance. The sluggish mien that the people had displayed in Vallarta had not been enlivened by the fiesta. Reflecting on this, Dan deduced that the death of General Garibay had been known about before they'd under-taken the journey.

Left of the corrals, and stretching back for at least a mile, flags on poles had been hammered into the ground, thereby marking the boundaries of a racetrack. It had been Dan's experience that every Mexican enjoyed horse-racing, not from the aspect of gambling but simply from their love of horses. Yet despite the distance by which he and Inez were separated from the crowd it was clear that all usual behaviour had been abandoned. Making judgements, arguing the merits of the riders and watching the animals perform to their utmost always brought a grin to the face of even the poorest peon. On this day, however, it was clear that there was little in the way of conversation between the groups scattered along the trackside. Gaps had been established between each family, as though every man was reluctant to speak to his neighbour.

Dan's musing that the fiesta was being attended by reluctant visitors was interrupted by Inez.

'That is Claudia Garibay,' she said, referring to the solitary figure in the courtyard. 'It was customary for the general and her to greet everyone as they arrived; then, when the events got under way, they would mingle with the crowds. Today she has remained in her seat.' After a pause she added, 'I wonder why she didn't call off the fiesta?'

'Perhaps it wasn't her decision,' said Dan. 'Let's go and find out, and remember to be as boyish as possible.'

★   ★   ★

Claudia Garibay's bearing was regal as she sat, statue-like, on the dais. Her back was straight and her chin high, but suffering showed on her face. The bruise on her temple and the gash on her cheek would account for physical pain and her features seemed also to reflect the mental anguish of mourning a dead husband.

When Dan and Inez approached she barely moved and, although she turned her head in his direction when Dan introduced himself, it was difficult to tell how much detail she absorbed. However, a remark about her husband's renown ignited a flame that flared angrily in her eyes. Although she remained silent it was obvious that she assumed Dan's words had been spoken facetiously: a malicious taunt from another American.

At that moment, two men approached, emerging from the shade of a porch from where they'd been keeping watch over Señora Garibay and those who spoke to her. They were Americans, armed and menacing as they strode across the courtyard in the direction of the dais.

'Who are you?' growled one of the men who hefted his rifle to impart the impression that he had some authority to question visitors to the compound. He was of average height and slim, and wore a short jacket that barely reached his waist so that it didn't hamper access to the big Colt that hung low on his right thigh.

'A visitor to the fiesta,' replied Dan. 'People in Vallarta said everyone was welcome and my friend here brought me along.'

'What business do you have in Vallarta?'

'Just passing through. Looking to buy some horses from one of the breeders hereabouts.'

The man was uneasy; he hadn't expected the arrival of an American, but apart from his in-built tendency to be cautious he could find no other cause for his suspicion. He cast a look at his companion who, blessed with less imagination, merely shrugged his acceptance of Dan's story. He wasn't even sure he understood why it had been necessary to leave the cool shade to confront the newcomer.

'You are missing the bullfight,' the man in the short jacket said.

'Not my idea of fun,' Dan told him.

'Then find something that is but don't hang around the courtyard. The house is out of bounds.'

Until now Claudia Garibay had been silent, as though all authority rested with the Americans, but when her soft voice uttered a few Spanish words they seemed to dispel that notion. However, when Dan turned to her it was clear that her words had been spoken to Inez who, too, had been silent and ignored. She stood with her head bowed so that under the large sombrero her face was completely hidden, but beneath her poncho there was movement that alarmed Dan.

His immediate thought was that she had drawn her gun and was preparing to shoot these men who were part of the gang that had attacked her home. When it became necessary he was prepared for a gunfight, but he had hoped to avoid it until he had Luis safe and Dick Lazarus in his sights. Then he relaxed, her arms dropped to her sides revealing empty hands.

The American growled at Señora Garibay. 'What did you say?'

'I was welcoming our visitors. That is why I'm here, is it not? Now I shall return to the house.' With those final words, Claudia Garibay arose and walked away across the courtyard.

Dan and Inez, too, quit the courtyard and headed off in the direction of the corrals, as though eager to see the events that were being staged there. As soon as they were out of earshot, Dan wanted to know what Claudia Garibay had told Inez.

'She told me they didn't understand Spanish.'

Dan's face took on an expression of bewilderment.

'Why did she tell you that?'

'Because I showed her this.' Inez dipped a hand under her poncho and when she extracted it, it held the ring bearing the family crest, the one he had brought from her father. 'She recognized it immediately.'

'Did she say anything else?'

'No, but we now know that we can safely exchange messages.'

For any chance of exchanging information they had first to get close to Señora Garibay again. With this in mind and in pursuit of their original intention of finding a likely place where Luis Robles might be being held prisoner, they skirted the corrals until they were in a position to work their way around the rear of the compound buildings. They had seen no more Americans among those congregated at the various event sites, which Dan considered significant. Perhaps his earlier estimation of the remaining strength of Dick Lazarus's gang was accurate.

'Two posted near the general's corpse, two more in the compound to watch Señora Garibay and perhaps another two somewhere indoors to guard Luis. Six men to deal with.'

'Seven,' corrected Inez. 'There is Lazarus, too.'

Dan rued the fact that he'd given voice to his calculation, sensing that he'd conveyed to Inez the impression that he thought six men was a force he could easily overcome. There was no guarantee of success facing one man: he wasn't making light of facing six, merely relieved that it wasn't the whole gang. Luck would play a part if they were successful in rescuing Luis, but he'd always known that when they finally met up with Dick Lazarus there would be bloodshed.

Surreptitiously, he regarded Inez. She seemed cool, ready to take on anyone who stood between her and her brother. Reluctant though Dan was to have her involved in a violent gunfight he knew that he had no argument which would dissuade her from the coming fray. From the very beginning, before meeting him in San Miguel, she had been determined to fight it out with Dick Lazarus. It was a desire that hadn't waned. She looked at him at that moment, seemed to read his thoughts and tried to banish his thoughts with a half-smile.

'When we get in they won't know what's hit them,' she said.

'There may be a lot more than six in there,' warned Dan.

'Let's not keep them waiting.'

They had reached a door at the rear of the house. Inez opened it, drew her six-gun and stepped inside. Dan, similarly prepared, was close on her heels. They were in a short corridor with a closed door four yards ahead of them and an open door two yards to their right. Cautiously, backs pressed against the wall, they edged towards the open door. A brief inspection from the doorway supplied two pieces of information: this was the kitchen and, at present, no one was employed there.

They moved on to the next door. Although Dan put his ear to it he could hear nothing that resembled the sounds of occupation. Silently, he opened the door just enough to provide a narrow view of what lay beyond. The door led into an alcove set in the back wall of a large living room. When assured by the uninterrupted silence that he had not aroused the interest of any occupant, he stepped more boldly through the entrance-way, holding his gun high, a command for Inez to remain in the corridor.

The back part of the room where the alcove was situated was two steps higher than the larger, front part, and the ceiling a great deal lower. Dan attributed the latter feature to the existence of a wide staircase which rose centrally from the lower floor. Above him, and running the length of the back wall there existed, he deduced, a balcony that led to upper rooms and provided a view of the room below. Gut instinct warned him that the balcony would be an ideal lookout post.

His eyes began to sweep the room from right to left, noting the fine furnishings, art objects and the presence of a grand piano. As his gaze reached a window he could see the dais where Claudia Garibay had sat and, more worryingly, he could see the two Americans who had confronted him earlier. For the moment they weren't a problem, their attention was fixed on events outside the house, but he knew he couldn't forget about them; if he could see them, then when they turned their heads they would be able to see him.

It was while he was contemplating this predicament that he heard the cough. It was a slight sound to his left, from that part of the room that he had not yet studied. The cough sounded again, a dry sound, and when he swung his head in that direction he saw her. Claudia Garibay, sitting on a high-backed chair beside a small writing table, was looking at him. At first Dan thought the look in her eyes signified alarm, as though he was an intruder come to harm her, but from somewhere she produced a small, lace-bordered handkerchief which she held to her face. She coughed once more, and the manner in which she fluttered the handkerchief told him that she was offering a warning, that she was telling him to advance no further. She got to her feet and began to move in his direction.

Above him, Dan heard the scuffing sound of a moving chair, then a challenging voice. 'Where are you going?'

'To get a drink of water.'

'There's wine in that flask. Drink that.'

'This is my home,' said Claudia Garibay. 'I'll drink what I choose.'

'Your home!' It was a malevolent chuckle that carried to Dan. 'That depends upon how nice you are to the boss when he returns.'

Claudia Garibay didn't respond but maintained her walk towards the door through which Dan Calloway was backing. The guard's words, however, were lodged in Dan's mind. Dick Lazarus wasn't here.

With the door to the corridor closed

behind her, Claudia Garibay spoke quickly and in a hushed tone. She had recognized Inez and had been hoping for someone to come on behalf of the Robles family ever since her brother had been brought to her home as a prisoner. But they were too late, she informed them, a ransom had been agreed and Lazarus had quit the compound an hour earlier with two men and Luis. When questioned further she had to tell them that she didn't know where the exchange was to take place.

Dan and Inez agreed that the logical location was someplace en route to her home. With fresh horses, overtaking Lazarus before the exchange was made was a possibility.

'Please,' pleaded Claudia Garibay, 'I need help. They murdered my husband and are holding my children as prisoners. They will be frightened. Help me to free them. There is no one else I can turn to.'

The desire of Inez Robles to set off in

pursuit of Dick Lazarus was clear. Her agitated body movements and facial expressions betrayed her anxiety. That she didn't give voice to her need to be once more in the saddle and eating up the miles between herself and the man who had attacked her home was testament to her concern for Claudia Garibay's situation, but Dan could feel the mental pull of the Mexican girl's need. They had been together for three days and had covered many miles; he too was anxious to bring the pursuit to a conclusion.

The story told by Claudia Garibay's face, however, couldn't be ignored. The bruises he could see were, he knew, only a small part of the violence, physical and mental, that she had endured. A murdered husband and captive children were heavy loads to carry, but the belief that she had no source of help other than from a foreign stranger showed that she had reached a level of desperation that couldn't be ignored.

'How many of Lazarus's men are still here?' he asked.

'Six,' she told him. 'There are two on the balcony where they can watch me and keep guard on the room where my children are held.'

Dan and Inez had already come into contact with the other four and the fact that they were split into pairs meant that, with a bit of luck, they could be treated as three separate targets. Inez was glaring at Dan, on the verge of telling him that they couldn't delay their departure, that they could come back to help Señora Garibay.

But Dan was thinking that fresh horses would benefit them when they continued their pursuit, and they could only do that if they dealt with those gang members who had been left at the hacienda. After explaining this to Inez he asked Claudia Garibay where her children were being held.

The room was almost directly above where they were standing, with a window that opened at the rear of the building.

'There is a ladder,' Claudia Garibay told him. 'I will keep the guards on the balcony in conversation while you rescue the children. When you have them safe I will join you and we'll flee together before the children are missed.'

Dan thought her idea sounded too simple but he didn't have time to refine it. If he was going to help her it had to be done immediately. Having found the ladder and propped it against the wall under the window he told Claudia Garibay to return to the house and Inez to stand guard. Claudia wished him luck and stepped back into the corridor. Inez was less willing to do his bidding.

The scowl on her face told Dan that she disapproved of his decision. Her words, however, proved that she wasn't without empathy for the Garibay family.

'Let me go up the ladder. Already, the children are afraid. You can't expect them to open the window to another American.'

Dan conceded the point but at that moment the matter lost its importance.

Voices sounded from the corridor, among them Señora Garibay's in protest against that of an insistent American. Suddenly, having been pushed, Claudia Garibay stumbled backwards from the open door and sprawled on the ground.

'What have you been doing out here?' asked the American as he emerged, lingering leeringly over the stricken woman. His interest in her disappeared almost at once: the realization that other people were present took him by surprise and in another moment he had recognized Dan.

'You,' he muttered and was about to ask his business at the back of the house when he saw the ladder and understood the implication instantly.

He swung the rifle he was carrying in an arc towards Dan but Claudia Garibay distracted him by throwing a handful of dust and grit at his face. Even so, he pulled the trigger and a bullet flew high into the air. Dan reached for his pistol but another gun fired first. The poncho worn by Inez Robles bulged as the bullet from the gun she held under it ploughed forward into the outlaw's chest. He toppled backwards, struggled to retain his feet, but Inez fired again and he dropped to the ground, dead.

Dan had hoped to rescue the children without fuss. Gunfire was certain to alert the other gang members, a fact corroborated by a rattle caused by the opening of an upper window. The second upstairs guard, more curious than apprehensive, peered out.

'What's all the shooting about, Zack?' he asked, but the last word almost died on his lips when he spotted his comrade stretched out on his back, eyes wide and blood soaking through his shirt. The second guard brought his rifle to his shoulder just as a bullet fired by Inez smashed the glass of the open window. Dan's shot was more accurate, smacking into the man's forehead, flinging him backwards and out of sight of those on the ground.

There had been too many shots fired

for the two who had accosted them by the dais not to be prepared for a fight. Their most direct route was through the house, but it was possible that they would adopt a pincer movement, perhaps forsaking the direct route altogether and approaching from each side of the building. There was no cover available for Dan and Inez so they followed Claudia Garibay into the corridor. Once inside, they heard someone blundering through the front room.

Worried about her children, Claudia Garibay ran forward, intending to intercept any other outlaw from reaching their room. Passing through the door into the alcove she was greeted by the gruff voice of the man in the short jacket, demanding to know the reason for the shooting and what had happened to the men who were supposed to be on guard on the balcony.

Señora Garibay was unable to form an answer, her eyes lifting to the room above, showing her concern for her children, who were still imprisoned. The gunman's eyes glanced in that direction also; he recognized the woman's weakness and headed for the stairs.

'It'll be a pity if they get in the line of fire,' he told her, 'but that's what's likely to happen if someone is trying to rescue them.'

Claudia Garibay ran to intercept him, reached the steps and grabbed him as he began to climb the stairs. He swung a hand at her, caught her a blow on the brow which caused her knees to buckle, but didn't force her to release the grip she had on his sleeve. He shook her, put his foot on her stomach and pushed her away. With a cry of desperation because now she was unable to hang on to his arm, she tumbled down the two stairs she'd climbed.

The man in the short jacket had almost reached the top of the flight when Dan's voice called to him.

'Hold it there,' he commanded.

The outlaw turned, rifle grasped in both hands, and fired a shot through the balustrade in Dan's direction. Dan returned fire, his bullet lifting a chunk of wood from the banister, causing it to ricochet away from its intended target. The outlaw fired again, a hasty shot that didn't threaten his opponent's life but which gave him time to seek cover behind one of the chairs that had recently been occupied by the guards. Dan stood his ground, waiting for the opportunity to get a clear shot at the outlaw.

It was Claudia Garibay who brought about the climax to the fight. With a sob she ran up the stairs, determined to reach her children before the gunman did. Dan yelled to her but she ignored him. Her impetus carried her to the top of the stairs and across the balcony towards the locked door behind which her children waited.

The gunman, bemused by her foray, turned his attention to her and, with a laugh, fired at the door, putting the children in mortal danger. Claudia screamed. Dan Calloway seized the opportunity that had been offered to him. In turning to fire at the door, the outlaw had exposed his side. Holding back the trigger, Dan fanned the hammer of his revolver until it was clacking on empty chambers. Each bullet struck home and the man in the short jacket pitched forward, to lie dead on the floor of the balcony.

While Claudia Garibay searched for the key that would release her children Dan set about the task of reloading his weapon. Footsteps sounded in the corridor, which Dan attributed to Inez but when he turned he found himself under the gun of the fourth outlaw. His own gun was useless as he was still in the process of loading it. The man pulled back the hammer and took aim.

It was the last thing he did. Behind him, Inez Robles fired first, the impact of the bullet thrusting him forward to lie still and bloody at Dan's feet.

Inez followed him into the room, her face grey and drawn as she looked down at the body.

'I heard him outside,' she said, 'coming in at the back to catch us in a trap, so I hid in the kitchen until he passed.'

'You came to my rescue again,' said Dan. 'It's becoming a habit.'

'You don't mind, do you?'

He gripped her upper arm and pulled her forward so that he could place a gentle kiss on her cheek. It was a kiss without any fire of passion but it held a promise which, for the moment, was all the answer she needed.

12

The sound of gunfire swiftly brought to an end the lacklustre interest of those attending the fiesta. Events dwindled to a halt and the people stood around, unsure what action to take. Those with children gravitated towards the far corral where the activities designated for children had been sited. The men looked at each other, seeking a leader, but everyone was reticent until the cause of the fight and its outcome were established. All were aware of the reputation of Dick Lazarus and his men and knew that they killed for pleasure. Even those who, before this day, had not come into contact with the outlaw band had only to look at the hill where the body of General Garibay was hanging to know the evil capabilities of the gang.

General Garibay had been a figure-head to the local community and they had been shocked by the coldblooded manner of his killing. The story of his murder, the capture of his children and the brutal abuse of his wife had circulated rapidly but no resistance had been organized because everyone was in fear that their own family would suffer a similar fate.

Lazarus, it was reported, had seen the general's home and wife and wanted both. Possession of the hacienda would provide a legitimate reason for being in Mexico and sanctuary from Texas lawmen. As long as his crimes in Mexico were directed against those who were enemies of the current government, he knew he would not be troubled by the authorities.

When the gunfire ceased, the more inquisitive men made their way to the compound to learn what they could about the fight. When they saw Señora Garibay reunited with her children they greeted them with shouts of joy. The happy sounds were soon echoed by others, eventually attracting everyone to the compound.

Their attention drawn by the activity within the compound, the two outlaws posted near the body of General Garibay watched from their high vantage point. The sound of the gunfight had not carried to them so, as they leant against a high rock, they assumed that the assembly within the walls was an established part of the annual fiesta. The grubby, bulky man used an eyeglass to survey the scene below. The sight of the woman with her children surprised him, but when he told his companion what he could see his voice held no hint of concern. Whatever was happening below was, he was sure, something that had been agreed before the boss departed; the possibility that the authority of Dick Lazarus had been ended never occurred to him.

'Riders coming,' he said.

The riders were Dan and Inez on the fresh horses that they'd acquired from the Garibay stock. Inez had cast aside the poncho and her slim figure drew the man's interest.

'What have we here?' he muttered. As the riders approached, he stepped on to the road with an upraised hand.

'Haul up there,' he shouted, and Dan and Inez pulled their mounts to a halt. As he walked towards the girl, the bulky man's malicious intention glittered in his eyes. 'I don't remember you,' he said.

'Of course you do,' she replied.

'I would have remembered if you'd passed here when you arrived.'

'I was wearing a poncho,' she told him.

'Oh yeah?' he said, casting a quick look at Dan and recalling the quiet Mexican who had been with him. 'Keeping yourself hidden, eh?'

'Yes. Do you like what you see?' Her question hinted that she was pleased to be attractive to him.

'Sure do,' he told her.

Bending at the waist, she leant down from the saddle so that her face was close to his.

'Then perhaps you'll like this,' she

whispered, 'because I kept it hidden also.' The smile on his face disappeared as he felt the prick of her knife point at his throat. 'Now drop that rifle.'

The other outlaw, at first distracted by the exchange between his companion and Inez, began to raise his rifle but halfway through the act he realized that he was under Dan Calloway's gun.

'Drop it,' said Dan. It didn't take more than a moment's thought for the man to comply. 'Now,' continued Dan, 'if you want to keep your lives, tell me where Dick Lazarus has arranged to pick up the ransom money.'

There was silence. Fear and loathing showed on the face of the bulky man at the point of the knife, the features of the other looked thoughtful and calculating.

'If you're hoping for help from those down at the compound,' Dan advised the pair, 'then you'll have a long wait. They are all dead. And just so you know,' he told the bulky man, 'she killed two of them.'

'We don't know where Lazarus is,' offered the thinner man.

'Then you have nothing to bargain with. That's a pity.'

'He's gone to the deserted monastery of San Bernadino. That's where the exchange will take place.' The burly man's words were uttered in a strangled, tense manner, because he valued his life. Inez had pricked his flesh with the point of her knife, had drawn blood, and the man was now anxious lest any awkward movement should result in his throat being pierced or slashed.

'Leave your guns on the ground, get on your horses and don't stop riding until you've crossed the Rio Grande. Don't come back to Mexico. They'll be coming soon to cut down General Garibay. I suspect if those people catch you they'll hang you up in his place.'

The men unfastened their gun-belts, mounted their horses and rode away.

'Do you know the deserted monastery of San Bernadino?' Dan asked Inez.

'Yes. It is not far from my home.'

They put spurs to their horses and were soon eating up the miles.

* * *

Lazarus, Claudia Garibay had informed them, had two men with him, one of whom was driving the flat-board wagon which transported Luis. Although the outlaw leader was ahead of them by more than an hour, his progress was restricted to the speed of the wagon. Dan and Inez, meanwhile, with fresh mounts under them, could set their own pace. Inez estimated that by demanding the utmost from their horses they could complete the journey in little more than two hours. With luck they would catch up to their quarry before the exchange was made. Neither Inez nor Dan were confident that Dick Lazarus would hand over his prisoner alive.

It was a hot, dirty ride with the dust and grit of the Chihuahuan desert adding to their discomfort. Although they covered the lower parts of their faces with neckerchiefs to prevent the sand entering their mouths and nostrils, they could do nothing but endure the stings and irritations caused by the sand against their exposed skin and eyes. But neither rider offered a word of annoyance, nor were they prepared to slacken the pace to alleviate the torment.

They had been riding for an hour, had been following the tracks of a wagon which they believed was the one transporting Luis to the monastery, when the girl called a halt.

'We can swing away from the road here,' she told Dan. 'West of here,' she pointed to the high sandstone buttes off to their right, 'there is a trail through a canyon that is too narrow and uneven for a wagon to use. We'll save several miles.'

It suited Dan to use an alternative route because the flattish land of the desert made it easy for Lazarus to spot someone on his back trail.

'How much farther is it to the monastery?'

'Thirty or forty minutes if we cut through the canyon.'

Running a horse until it dropped wasn't Dan's usual practice and at this moment he would have preferred to give them a few minutes' rest, but he scoured the country ahead and could see no sign of those of whom they were in pursuit. They had to push on as quickly as possible. Inez had already turned her animal towards the high ground, so he tapped the flanks of his own and followed in her tracks.

The canyon, which climbed steadily, was indeed unsuitable for a wheeled vehicle. Its mile-long floor was littered with rocks and boulders and at one point it narrowed to such an extent that it became wide enough only for the passage of one horse, but when they emerged they were on a ridge which gave them a view over the seemingly endless desert scrub. Inez pointed ahead to the stark, irregular outline of the monastery ruins and pulled down the neckerchief that covered the lower part of her face. An expression of satis-faction showed as she looked at Dan.

'We've beaten them,' she said.

Dan was still surveying the scene, needing to be more certain that they were ahead of Dick Lazarus before celebrating their arrival at the monastery. However, a moment later, he nodded his agreement. Nothing appeared to be moving, there was no evidence that either Dick Lazarus or the representatives of Inez's family were heading towards the ruins. For a moment this disturbed Dan, fearing that they had been duped once more, that the exchange wasn't to take place at the ruins, but he recalled the tracks they'd followed and that know-ledge soothed away his doubts.

'Look.' Inez drew Dan's attention to dust rising in the west. 'Two riders,' she said. 'They must be bringing the ransom money.'

Although the scrubland they were look-ing across appeared flat, it consisted of mounds and dips behind which or into which men could disappear for several minutes. So it had been with the men now heading in the direction of the ruined monastery and, Dan suspected, it also accounted for the outlaws' approach coming from the opposite direction. A minute later, perhaps a mile distant and rising from an arroyo, the appearance of a wagon and accompanying outrider proved him correct.

'What do we do?' asked Inez.

Dan had no clear plan. If, as he assumed, Dick Lazarus was keeping Luis alive only long enough to draw those carrying the money into his clutches, then whatever action they took had to happen quickly. He could sense the mix of emotions by which the Mexican girl was gripped. Her words had been uttered quickly, a sign that she believed that the activity of the past few days was coming to a conclusion, that her brother was close at hand and that she couldn't wait to set him free.

Dan worried that she was underestimating the danger that Dick Lazarus and his men presented. They weren't going to hand over their prisoner and ride away. In a few minutes some people would be dead; if they were reckless the likelihood was that he and Inez would be counted among them. Concern for the safety of Inez Robles was predominant in his mind. For days he had tried to chase her away from the coming confrontation; now that it was at hand the thought that she might be hurt or killed churned in his guts. But, no matter how much he pleaded, he knew she wouldn't stay out of the fight and, more worryingly, he knew that he needed her help.

'We need to get them in a crossfire,' he said. 'You make a dash for the monastery and cover the outlaws with your rifle. By taking advantage of the uneven ground you ought to be able to make the ruins without being seen. I'll get as close as possible on this side of the road. Don't fire until I do. If possible we'll wait until the exchange has been completed. When you fire, shoot to kill.'

It wasn't an instruction he enjoyed giving the girl but he knew that if there was a fight it would be to the death. He watched for a moment as she began the ride down the ridge; then, after checking the location of the advancing parties, he too began the descent.

A low mound twenty yards from the monastery walls provided cover for Dan. He tried to espy Inez but could not. Although he was eager to see her and confirm that she'd reached the ruins without mishap, he was pleased to think that she had found a station that was so well obscured from the road. Lying flat with his rifle stretched out before him, he watched the approach of the two parties.

An elderly Mexican, the *segundo* of the Robles ranch, dressed in black with silver decoration, rode side by side with another Mexican who was leading a saddled horse. The second man was younger, slim and keen-eyed. On a slight rise fifty yards from the walls they halted, waiting for the wagon that was moving slowly towards them.

When they were separated by a hundred yards the wagon driver pulled the horse to a halt. His companion climbed from his horse on to the wagon and, with the aid of the driver, dragged upright a figure that had been lying on the bed of the wagon. The figure was bound, his hands behind his back, and he had to be held by the two outlaws to prevent him from falling, but it was clearly Luis. Despite showing obvious signs of maltreatment it was none the less clear that he was alive.

In response and in recognition that the captive was the person they'd been sent to ransom, the old Mexican lifted his saddle bags high, a gesture to show the outlaws that he had brought the money that had been demanded for the release of Luis, and also to signal that the exchange could now take place.

Luis was dropped on to the wagon floor, the driver got back on his seat. With a shout to his team he urged them forward. The second man climbed on to his horse with an easy step into a stirrup and an agile swing of his leg. It was a movement that prompted a thought — and warning bells — in Dan's mind.

Dick Lazarus, he had been told, had quit Claudia Garibay's hacienda with two of his men. According to Inez, Lazarus was a big man with a scar on his face. That description matched neither of the outlaws he could see. Where, he wondered, was the man he had crossed and recrossed the Rio Grande to find?

At that moment, with the gap between captors and liberators closing, a commotion drew the attention of everyone to the monastery ruins.

★ ★ ★

Not for a moment had Inez Robles considered confessing to Dan Calloway that she was nervous at the prospect of facing Dick Lazarus. For days she had steeled herself for this encounter, but now that it was imminent she found herself beset by doubts and cares. Her care was for the safety of Dan Calloway and her brother; her doubts centred around her ability to be of help to the big American. Throughout the past days she had doggedly refused to leave him but now, at the most critical moment, she was losing confidence in herself. She couldn't bear the prospect of being a hindrance when he needed her most.

As she rode downhill she was surprised to find that her face was wet. While wiping it dry with her sleeve she remembered the need to remain unobserved; she hoped that she hadn't inadvertently exposed herself to the distant outlaws. Eventually, by a circuitous route, she reached the ruins from the rear. She dismounted and tethered her horse; it snickered gently. For a moment she was startled by an answering whinny and she looked around nervously. Then, although it had seemed closer, she figured the sound had come from one of the animals that were heading her way. Silently she chastized herself for being jumpy and knew that she had to regain the determination that had brought her this far.

At a stooped run, ensuring she remained hidden by even the lowest wall, she darted among the ruins until she'd reached a point that gave her an unobstructed view of the road. Kneeling, she watched the wagon approach, and coming from the west she recognized Pedro Alvarez and his son, Tonio, who had been born and had grown up on the Robles ranch.

Now the sight of her brother, bound, beaten and propped between his captors, renewed her anger and revitalized her resolve to see him returned safely to his home. She raised her rifle, rested it on the wall and, with the sights fixed on the chest of the man riding alongside the wagon, she squinted along the barrel. In her opinion he was the one most likely to act as her brother's executioner in the event of trouble.

It was possibly at the same moment that it occurred to Dan Calloway that the absence of Dick Lazarus troubled Inez; it was also at that moment that one hand grabbed the barrel of her rifle while another covered her mouth and dragged her away from the wall.

Preparing an ambush for the Robles riders had always been a part of Dick Lazarus's plan, and as Dan Calloway had suspected, keeping Luis alive had only been a means to draw the liberators within easy range of his guns. So he had ridden ahead, found a suitable spot from which to execute his deadly plan and was smoking a black cigarillo when his horse responded to the snickering of another. He had spotted the Mexican girl's progress and, as she knelt, preparing to strike against his men, he identified her as his prisoner's sister. With his superior strength it was easy for him to drag her away from the wall, wrest the rifle from her grip and cast it aside.

Inez struggled but his big, rough

hand was clamped tightly against her face. Swiftly, he spun her around and slapped her hard, laughing as he did so. He dragged her towards the road, yelling at Pedro Alvarez that his ambush plan had failed and that they would all die.

The wagon driver stopped his team, suddenly and violently, so that the bits snagged the mouths of the front animals, causing them to rear in their traces. The rider went for his pistol, pulling his horse behind the wagon, making it clear that Luis was his target. Tonio too, pushing his mount forward so that he was in front of his father, went for his gun.

Indecision caused a hesitant reaction from Dan Calloway. His immediate thought was to save Inez from the violence of Dick Lazarus. Subconsciously, however, he knew that Luis was in the most imminent danger and that he was in the best position to save him. He fired once, the bullet striking the rider in the chest, throwing him over his horse's tail on to the ground beyond.

A yell reached Dan's ears as he turned his attention to the attack on Inez. The shout had come from Dick Lazarus, who was staggering away from the girl with blood seeping from a long slash that stretched from the fingers of his left hand almost to the elbow. He cursed Inez, cursed the knife she had mysteriously produced, and clutched with his right hand for the pistol holstered on his thigh. Dan didn't give him time to draw it. Three bullets struck Dick Lazarus in the chest, pitching him to the ground, dead.

Dan hurried to join Inez who was standing over the outlaw chief's body.

'I will cut out his heart,' she said, and, although her hand was shaking, Dan believed her. Keeping his voice as gentle as possible he swayed her from her intention.

'Leave him there,' he told her. 'The vultures will do the job for you. Luis is more in need of your attention.'

The fight had been brief and one-sided. The outlaws hadn't fired a shot but two of them were dead and the Lazarus gang was destroyed for ever. The wagon driver, who had had no opportunity to draw a weapon, had thrown up his hands in surrender as soon as he had been able to bring the wagon to a standstill. In similar fashion to the treatment of the outlaw survivors at Claudia Garibay's hacienda, his life was spared on the understanding that he never returned to Mexico.

★   ★   ★

Reunited with her brother, Inez set about treating the cuts and bruises he had sustained and, free from the threat of death, Luis soon found a glimmer of his usual good humour. None the less, he was overwhelmed by his sister's devotion when details of her search for him were disclosed.

Pedro Alvarez broke the good news to Luis that his father had not been killed in the attack. It was time, he said, to make the journey home. Luis wasn't yet ready to ride a horse so he lay in the wagon. Dan Calloway mounted his horse and drew alongside the wagon. He tipped his hat in farewell.

'Where are you going?' asked Inez.

'Back along the Tonto Rim,' he said. 'There are horses to find. Some of them are my property.'

'Then I'm going, too,' she declared. 'We're trail partners, aren't we?'

'Sure,' he answered, 'but sometimes we have different tasks.'

'Most of those horses are our property,' she said.

'I know, but at the moment, your job is to get your brother safely home.'

'Pedro and Tonio can do that.'

'Tonio is coming with me to round up the stock.'

'You'll come back with him?'

'It would be difficult to marry you if I didn't come back.'

A slow smile touched her face, replacing the small lines of concern that had formed on her brow. 'You want to marry me?'

'Figure I've got to if I want to discover your secret.'

'What secret?'

'Where *do* you keep that knife?'

FURY AT BENT FORK

B. S. Dunn

What becomes known as the Stone Creek Valley war starts with one word: Guilty. Eager to get their hands on his father's ranch, the Committee — the four biggest ranchers in the area — send Chad Hunter to jail on a trumped-up charge of cattle rustling. Upon his release a year later, he's got his work cut out for him, with the Committee's hired thugs terrorizing the area. When his brother is lynched and his father shot down, Hunter loads his guns and prepares to deal out his own brand of justice . . .

KID PALOMINO: OUTLAWS

Michael D. George

Outlaw Bill Carson and his gang ride into Fargo knowing that the sheriff and his deputies are out of town. Carson has inside information about the bank and banker, which the ruthless killer intends to use to his advantage. What Carson and his equally bloodthirsty gang do not know is that the deputies have returned early. Kid Palomino and his fellow lawman Red Rivers notice the strangers in town and decide to find out who they are. All hell erupts as the lawmen confront the outlaws . . .

THE GUNSMOKE SERENADE

Thomas McNulty

While passing through Cherrywood Crossing, US Marshal Maxfield Knight is confronted by a gang of hired guns who tell him to ride the other way, or be shot down. With no choice but to ride into the high country, Knight soon learns he is being hunted by a man named Silas Manchester, but why, he has no idea. Determined to survive this dangerous game, and aided by a mountain man named Lacroix, Knight decides to bring the fight to Manchester and get answers . . .

INCIDENT AT PEGASUS HEIGHTS

I. J. Parnham

When fossil-hunter Jim Dragon goes to the aid of a woman in distress, Elmina Fay, his precious fossils are stolen from him in the process. Jim vows to reclaim his property and Elmina offers to help him, but only if he'll do something for her. She has heard that the bones of a winged horse have been found nearby, and she wants him to bring them to her. Jim is about to discover that the truth behind the tale is even stranger than he could have imagined . . .

THE McCALLUM BOYS

C. J. Sommers

Most folks either love or hate the McCallum boys. Everyone fears them. Their father brought them up to Wyoming from Texas and died, leaving them half-grown and rough-tempered. To their neighbours on the Porter ranch, Rose Ann and her niece Becky, the McCallum boys are helpful, attentive and polite. When Rose Ann hires a man from Medicine Bow to drive her horse herd to market, she discovers he has more on his mind for her and Becky than a few chores — but he has not yet met the McCallum boys . . .